"You allow me to get this far, lady—"

Rolf was coldly angry now. "You allow me to get this far before you start putting up the barriers? And 'no right'? Where do rights come into it, into the relationship between a man and a woman these days? And 'no connection between us,'" he quoted her bitingly, "when there's this electricity whenever we touch, this pull? For me, it overrides everything else, every other consideration."

He spoke the truth—she could not deny it—but how could she tell him it was exactly that "pull" that made her so afraid? She found it—him—so irresistible that she could hardly bring herself not to fling her arms around his neck every time he ended a kiss and beg for another, and another....

Dear Reader,

We know from your letters that many of you enjoy traveling to foreign locations—especially from the comfort of your favorite chair. Well, sit back, put your feet up and let Harlequin Presents take you on a yearlong tour of Europe. **Postcards from Europe** will feature a special title every month, set in one of your favorite European countries, written by one of your favorite Harlequin Presents authors. This month, come with us to Switzerland. Located at the heart of the Alps and the very heart of Europe, Switzerland is a fitting setting for this wonderful love story!

The Editors

P.S. Don't miss the fascinating facts we've compiled about Switzerland. You'll find them at the end of the story.

HARLEQUIN PRESENTS
Postcards from Europe

LILIAN PEAKE

No Promise of Love

Harlequin Books

TORONTO • NEW YORK • LONDON
AMSTERDAM • PARIS • SYDNEY • HAMBURG
STOCKHOLM • ATHENS • TOKYO • MILAN
MADRID • WARSAW • BUDAPEST • AUCKLAND

ISBN 0-373-11700-0

NO PROMISE OF LOVE

Copyright © 1994 by Lilian Peake.

This edition published by arrangement with Harlequin Enterprises B.V.

® and TM are trademarks of the publisher. Trademarks indicated with
® are registered in the United States Patent and Trademark Office, the
Canadian Trade Marks Office and other in countries.

Printed in U.S.A.

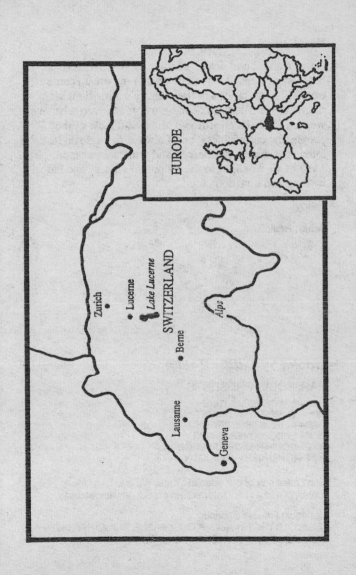

Dear Reader,

It was a childhood dream of mine to visit Switzerland, but it wasn't until I was married that my dream came true. My expectations of the country's attractions were more than fulfilled. Since then, we've returned whenever we can. I love its cleanliness, the friendliness of the people, the colorfulness, and I always feel safe on its integrated, finely engineered and punctual transport. Most of all, I delight in the mountain scenery and the inviting and nutritious food.

Enjoy!

Lilian Peake

Books by Lilian Peake

HARLEQUIN PRESENTS

1268—DANCE TO MY TUNE
1316—CLIMB EVERY MOUNTAIN
1485—IRRESISTIBLE ENEMY
1532—UNDERCOVER AFFAIR
1580—GOLD RING OF REVENGE
1629—STRANGER PASSING BY

CHAPTER ONE

IT WAS not until the aircraft started its descent that Abigail began to wonder if she should have been on that flight at all. Or any flight, for that matter.

When the senior architect for whom she had been working had retired, and his successor in the same practice had, on his promotion, insisted on bringing with him his own secretary, Abigail had watched her own job disintegrate before her very eyes.

'I'm deeply sorry,' George Alwyn had told her, 'but there seems to be nothing I can do to help you remain in this firm.'

'I do understand, Mr Alwyn,' Abigail had told him, heart sinking, 'and I also appreciate and thank you for all that you've done on my behalf, especially for the very helpful sum you've negotiated as my redundancy pay.'

He had smiled and nodded, and turned his attention to other matters.

Abigail had not, however, really 'understood', and she had said as much to Raymond Felder, the young man whose room was next to hers in the rented house they shared with two others in the suburbs of London.

'So——' he had lifted a shoulder '—use the money they're giving you to take a holiday. I know. . .' He had jumped up from her bed—her room, like the others, possessed only one chair, and she was occupying that—and roamed around, pausing to frown at the back gardens of the houses backing on to the one they all shared. 'Come back with me to my home country. To Switzerland, to my land of mountains and lakes, and——' he grimaced '—where the views are far better than that one out there.'

'I couldn't possibly afford it,' Abigail had answered

promptly, 'but thanks for the suggestion. One day, maybe, if I ever get a job again.'

'No, no, you would come to Lucerne as my guest.' He faced her, his bright, intelligent features lighting up. 'In fact, as the family's guest. You see, we live in a hotel. There is a house which is being renovated for us—my father, my brother, my sister and myself—but until it is ready we are residing in the Hotel Panorama Grand.'

Abigail sighed. 'Sounds great, Raymond, but I couldn't possibly accept. How could I wish myself on to your family when I haven't even met them? Your mother——'

He shook his head sadly. 'We lost her a few years ago.'

'I'm very sorry. Well,' she continued after a pause, 'your father, then, not to mention your brother——'

'Don't mention *him*. He's nine years older than I am. . .'

Which, Abigail calculated, made him a little over thirty, six years older than herself.

'And he thinks that gives him the right to boss me around and to throw his weight about generally. He has this deep-seated prejudice against the opposite sex, too.'

'Well,' Abigail laughed, 'since women make up half the population of the world, he must be spending most of the time with a frown on his face.'

'Don't get me wrong,' Raymond took her up. 'He appreciates everything a woman has to offer. You know?' He made a few curving gestures in the air. 'It's really because the woman he was all set to marry left him for a three-times-over millionaire. He and Beatrice were both very young and she was his first love, and she hurt him so deeply, he said, that he's sworn no woman will ever get under his skin again. All they're out for is money and position, he says. Love, in his opinion, doesn't come into the female scheme of things.' As Abigail made to express her anger at such inflexible prejudice on the brother's part Raymond went on, 'All the same —— ' he inspected his nails '—he has room for women in his life, and when I say room I mean *his* room.' He smiled. 'You get my meaning?'

'I'm glad, then,' Abigail asserted, 'that I won't ever be meeting him.'

'I didn't exactly say that.' He took her hand and put in hurriedly, 'But don't let that put you off coming. I shouldn't even have mentioned Rolf. It's true that you probably won't ever get to meet him. You see, the other passion in his life is his work. He is the head of an engineering company in Zurich, and all of his time is absorbed by his work; all the time, that is, that he can spare from his current lady friend. She's British, name of Laura Marchant, financial journalist, with a good brain, plus. . .well, you can guess, can't you? So even if my dear brother does put in an appearance, he probably wouldn't even notice your existence. Does that persuade you to come?'

Abigail still felt plagued by doubts, although why, she could not fathom. 'Will your sister be there?'

'Martina? Not at first, but later. She's a career girl, but she's—well, she's OK, too. Not hard, or anything. Fashion's her line—yes, clothes. She's away on business at the moment.'

Now, as Abigail fastened her seatbelt, and closed her eyes, wondering exactly what she had let herself in for, she wished she had not allowed Raymond to persuade her.

He had just completed a year's accountancy experience at his uncle's office in the heart of London. Delighted by her acceptance of his offer, Raymond had flown out in advance while Abigail had worked out her notice and put her affairs in order.

Her room had been let to another girl and it had been with a feeling of having burned her boats that she had left for the airport that morning, closing the door behind her with a sense of excitement, and also—she could not deny it—with a feeling of apprehension because, in view of her need to economise financially, she really should not be taking such a holiday.

No matter how willing Raymond had been to treat her as his 'guest', she simply couldn't accept his generosity and was determined to finance out of her own savings her stay in his country. Also, she consoled herself, the Hotel Panorama Grand was probably reasonably priced, otherwise how could the Felder family possibly afford to stay there indefinitely?

She had packed clothes sufficient for a short stay, but, even so, her two cases and shoulder-bag on the luggage trolley proved difficult to push. Raymond had promised to meet her, and it was with relief that she recognised his trim build and saw his smiling, good-looking face in the crowd.

They had known each other for a year, but there had been nothing but friendship, warm though it was, between them. And it had remained that way, despite Raymond's occasional attempts to break through her emotional barriers.

For some months Abigail had dated Des Casey, a junior member of the model-making staff. She had liked him a lot, but the 'more than liking' which he claimed he had felt towards her had fast melted away when a young woman architect had joined the firm.

Raymond, however, was sweet-natured and generous. His kisses were undemanding, and it was because of this that Abigail had found them easy to tolerate.

'Hey, Abigail,' Raymond would sometimes remark, 'I like you a lot. You like me, yes? OK, so why don't we. . .?' A sigh, then, 'No? So I'm good at waiting.' He had usually left it at that.

His greeting now was an enveloping hug and a kiss on both cheeks. 'Hey, it's good to see you again, Abby. OK, here we go. I know the train schedules by heart and if we make our way now we'll be in time for the next one. The station is below the airport, so we have to go down. Follow me.'

This Abigail did, wondering at Raymond's ability to weave the trolley which he had taken from her through the milling crowds.

'Look,' he commented with some pride as they

reached the escalator, 'how our luggage trolleys are so cleverly designed that they can be taken on the escalators.'

'That's just great,' Abigail commented, standing behind him as they descended, wondering at the way the wheels of the trolley locked themselves on to the moving stairs.

'Swiss engineers are clever devils, are they not?' Raymond joked, glancing at her over his shoulder. 'As I told you, my brother is one of them.' At the bottom he shoved the trolley hard on to level ground and continued pushing it, glancing at Abigail again as she walked beside him. 'I am glad,' he confided, 'that you have come.'

'Thanks,' she answered, moved by his words, 'and thank you for asking me.'

'Did you know — of course you don't, so I will tell you — ' he grinned, still pushing the trolley ' — that the industry that takes first place in my country is mechanical engineering?'

'But I thought. . .' She was a little breathless trying to keep up with him.

'Skiing, mountaineering, tourism?' He shook his head. 'They come a long way down. After engineering come the chemical and pharmaceutical industries, followed by textiles and, of course, who hasn't heard of Swiss watches?'

'Cheese and chocolate, too,' Abigail added with a smile. 'I've heard you talk about those quite often. Not to mention banking and insurance. . .'

'I think — ' he glanced over his shoulder with a smile ' — that you must have swallowed a guidebook on your way here. Now. . .' He changed course, manoeuvring the trolley with ease 'We must find our platform.'

Twenty minutes later they were seated together in an open compartment.

'Raymond?' Abigail asked, attracting his attention from the passing view. 'I'm worried. About the cost of the hotel room, about — '

'I told you. . .' He took her hand '. . . don't be.

You've come as my *guest*, Abby, which means I'll see to the cash angle of your holiday.'

'I won't allow you to,' Abigail declared. 'You can't possibly afford to pay for someone else's holiday. We've been out together enough for me to know that your pockets don't possess secret gold-mines.'

He laughed. 'You'd be surprised.'

It was when the taxi deposited them outside the hotel and Abigail saw how imposing it was that she exclaimed agitatedly, 'I'm sorry, Raymond, but I simply can't stay here.'

He put down her cases and turned to her, his expression comical. 'You mean it's not good enough for you?'

'Don't be silly. You know me better than that. I mean that not only can I not afford its prices — and it's obvious from just looking at it how high they are — but nor could I possibly stay here as your guest. It would cost you a fortune, too, and I know for certain that *you* couldn't afford that.'

He shook his head. 'You know nothing, Abigail. Shall I tell you a secret? The Hotel Panorama Grand belongs to the Felder family. No, don't look so stunned.'

She made to pick up her cases, but Raymond stopped her. 'Don't let it spoil our friendship,' he pleaded, then shook his head again. 'I don't know of any other girl who would run the other way when a guy told her he wasn't as poverty-stricken as she thought he was. Come on, Abby, of course you can stay here, especially now you know it won't really be me who's doing the paying?'

With a sigh she allowed him to take her cases from her. 'Just a few days, then.'

Raymond beamed. 'She's relented. She's put aside her great principles — for a few days, as you said. At least,' he amended in a whispered aside to an invisible listener as he led the way into the hotel reception area.

'You haven't seen my room yet,' Raymond said later that afternoon as they met in the corridor. 'It's a bit larger than yours, but not as big as my father's or brother's. It's not far, just along here.'

The room was indeed larger than her own and better furnished, but that, she thought, was to be expected. The bathroom contained many personal items, whereas hers contained a courtesy tray which, however, in the items offered was of a higher standard than those usually found in holiday hotels.

'Make yourself at home,' Raymond invited, 'while I fix us a drink.' He used a key to open a refrigerator. 'Alcoholic or non-alcoholic?'

'Non, please.'

Extracting two cans of Coke, he poured the contents of one into a glass and handed it to Abigail, tearing open the other and drinking from it, head back.

Finishing his drink, he took Abigail's empty glass, then opened a cupboard and pulled out a tray of cassettes.

'Darn,' he exclaimed. 'The one I want is missing. I'm sure I lent it to Rolf.' He replaced the tray and straightened. 'Want to see where my dear brother resides?' He produced a key from his drawer. 'It's two along from mine.'

His brother's suite was, as Raymond had said, slightly larger, but just as modern and well furnished.

'Bathroom,' Raymond gestured. 'Bedroom. Look around while I search. He's had the cassette for weeks.'

Abigail gazed at the view, lifting her eyes to the mountains beyond. Turning, she became aware of the masculine ambience, the darker colours, the bold patterns of the curtains, the books scattered around and leaning drunkenly against each other on a shelf.

Their subject matter, she noted, was mostly engineering, with power generation interspersed among them. One or two books, to her eyes strangely out of place, dealt with hotel management. There was not one indication that the occupant of the room possessed a brain that, even for an hour or so, relaxed into fiction and the imagined world.

On a small circular table near the window stood a

photograph of a woman. Her expression was confident,
as if she was certain of her place in the world—and in
this man's world in particular? Her hair was crisply
styled, emphasising the oval shape of her face, the low-
cut dress she wore revealing the graceful length of the
neck, and the promise of shapeliness beneath, yet
cleverly softening the faintly disdainful lift of the chin.

'Raymond?' Abigail indicated the picture.

'The lady? That is Laura, Laura Marchant, Rolf's
girlfriend. Didn't you guess? I did tell you about her.
And do you see what I mean when I said that my
brother appreciates womanly. . .*whew!*' Again his
hands expressed his meaning.

The possibility had occurred to her that it might have
been the elder brother's lady friend, but for some
inexplicable reason she had not wanted her suspicions
to be confirmed.

She wandered across to a closed door.

'Bathroom,' Raymond had informed her, still searching. 'Next to it is the bedroom. Go ahead, look inside.
Don't be scared. He's not likely to come in and catch
you in there. He's away, I told you.'

The bathroom was roomy but strictly masculine,
although Abigail did spy one or two feminine touches,
like a bottle of fragrant shampoo—her nostrils picked
it up—and an uncapped lipstick, which told tales to
which, for some unaccountable reason, Abigail immediately closed her mind.

The bed was large, the carpeting dark brown, the
curtains a brilliant, contrasting orange. Abigail could
almost sense the man's presence, and although she had
never met him she had the strangest feeling that she
had.

An unaccountable sensation of being watched filled
her with an inexplicable need to escape, and Abigail
quickly closed the bedroom door behind her, at which
moment the telephone rang in the living area.

'Raymond? Will you answer?' Abigail asked, staring
at the instrument as if it were a wild animal about
to spring.

Raymond was on his hands and knees, with his head inside his brother's storage cabinet.

'Be a pet and answer, will you?' came his muffled voice. 'Won't be important. Reception knows Rolf's away.'

Abigail lifted the receiver and, since she didn't know which language to use, just listened.

'Raymond?' The voice was deep and masculine, the tone just this side of ill-tempered. '*Warum bist du in meinem Zimmer*?'

'Who is it?' Raymond asked, withdrawing from the neat racks of audio cassettes.

'*Hello*?' The voice, angry now, came again. '*Bist du dort*?'

Silently Abigail shook her head, holding out the receiver.

Raymond scrambled to his feet and took it from her. 'Hallo? Rolf? *Ja, Ich bin hier.*' He listened, looked at Abigail, looked away. '*Ja, eine Frau. Sie ist Engländerin.* Her name? It is Abigail, Abigail Hailey. *Ja, sie ist meine. . .Freundin.* Friend. More than that?'

He hesitated, then talked on, taking refuge, Abigail was sure, in the fact that she would not be able to understand him. He nodded, following the action with a smug smile and a covert, appreciative glace at Abigail. He continued the conversation at some speed, appearing to explain the reason for his presence in the room, and Abigail's presence there, also.

It seemed to Abigail that the man at the other end of the line was not at all pleased. 'Get her out of here?' Raymond seemed deliberately to have changed back to English. 'OK, but she's doing no harm. She's not trying to seduce me or anything.'

'Raymond!' Abigail exclaimed, red-faced. 'Will you stop feeding your brother with misleading information about me?'

'Yes,' Raymond said to the caller, 'she is annoyed. *Ja*, with me. And maybe with you, who knows?' He ignored the exclamation, which seemed to be a growl

mixed in with a shout, so loud that it even reached
Abigail's ears.

The conversation continued, and when Abigail heard
Raymond say, '*Ja, Onkel Manfred ist OK*' she knew
that Raymond's brother was interrogating him as to his
year's work in their uncle's London office.

The discussion over, Raymond turned with a pained
expression.

'What's wrong,' he asked, 'with telling Rolf you're
my girlfriend? After all, you're a girl and my friend.
Are you not?' His arm around her shoulders pulled her
to him. 'My good friend. I like your kisses; you like
mine. And you like me. Yes?'

Abigail smiled. She did indeed like him a lot, but
there her feelings for him rested.

He knelt again, replacing the cassettes on their
respective shelves.

'Found it,' he exclaimed, waving a cassette in the air
and standing up. 'Now you will dine with me tonight,
yes.' It was not a question, and Abigail laughed.

'Thanks, that would be very nice. Now —— ' she went
to the door ' — I must organise myself.'

Raymond nodded. 'Until later, then. Seven-thirty.
It's a date.' He saw her to her room, then returned to
his own.

Abigail's flushed reflection frowned back at her. Just
hearing the elder brother's voice had upset her composure. She hadn't said a word to him, yet her heart
was thumping as if she had been engaged in a violent
argument with the man.

She looped her long dark hair behind her ears. Bright
lights of anger flecked her brown eyes, while her wide
mouth was taut, her oval-shaped face quite lacking in
its usual good humour. Her dark eyebrows were drawn
together, her faintly tip-tilted nose seeming to quiver at
the thought of Rolf Felder ordering her from his room.

Raymond was waiting when she stepped out of the
lift. 'Our table is ready. You look fine.'

Abigail glanced down at her cream blouse and loose

pink cotton trousers. 'I wasn't sure what to wear. I didn't know how formal——'

'You're just right,' Raymond assured her as he led the way across the restaurant towards the tall, wide windows. 'We like our guests to relax, not always to be on their best behaviour.'

The white tablecloth glowed red with the light from the glass-enclosed candle. Outside, the lake stretched into the evening mist, which veiled the distant beauty of the mountains.

Raymond picked up the two large menus, handing one to Abigail, and half disappeared behind his own. 'What is your choice for this evening? I think I fancy. . .let me see. . .'

'There's such a wide choice,' Abigail commented, 'that I'm finding it difficult to make up my mind.'

'Take it from me,' Raymond answered, 'it's all delicious. Did you know——' he put down the menu '——that Switzerland has an international cuisine? A so-called Swiss cuisine doesn't really exist. There are Swiss dishes, of course, many of them, but. . .' He resumed his perusal of the menu. 'This evening, how about *Bouillon mit Gemüse*, clear soup with vegetables? After helping ourselves, that is, to *Kaltes Vorspeisenbuffet*— cold dishes from the buffet.'

'Not both, surely?' Abigail protested.

'But of course, and that's only the start. For the main course there's a choice of dishes. No need to translate; it's in English also. Rump steak with tomatoes and peppers, or perch fillets with white wine sauce. Then comes the dessert——'

'Please,' Abigail protested, 'I couldn't possibly eat all that.'

'OK, so select what you want and we'll order, yes?'

It was over coffee at the end of the meal that Abigail told her companion of her decision. 'Thanks a million, Raymond, for offering to pay for my stay here, but I absolutely insist on paying for myself.' She smiled. 'And no arguments, please.'

He looked pained. 'Which means, I suppose, that you'll be booking out tomorrow.'

'The cost of staying here being so high, you mean?' She lifted a shoulder. 'A couple of days, maybe. It's not that I want to leave. Perhaps I could find somewhere near by that's less expensive?'

Raymond drained his cup and lowered it thoughtfully to the saucer. 'If we found you something useful to do, would that salve your conscience about accepting our hospitality?'

With a smile, Abigail asked, 'You mean washing dishes in the kitchen?'

Raymond laughed. 'Not quite, Abby. It's so stupid, and quite unnecessary, but if that conscience of yours insists. . . I'm thinking aloud. Ah, I have it. A vacancy here in the restaurant for a waitress——'

'There is?'

'Probably not, but one could be made. Or for an assistant at the bar. Or even. . .'

He looked at her doubtfully.

She helped him out. 'As I suggested, in the kitchens?'

'You wouldn't like that, Abigail, nor would I. It would be hard work, and I did invite you here as my guest.'

'I wouldn't mind the hard work, honestly, Raymond.'

He pushed away his coffee-cup. 'Will you leave it with me? In the meantime, will you *please* accept my offer of hospitality?'

Head on one side, he looked so appealing that she laughed and nodded.

'Good. Round one to me.' He poured them each some more coffee, then clinked his cup against hers. 'We will drink to that.'

Next morning, Abigail finished her breakfast, which she had taken at the table on her very own balcony.

The breeze was warm and a wonderful lethargy had her leaning back in the chair and closing her eyes. It had been so long since she'd had a holiday abroad that she had almost forgotten how to relax and let the world go by.

'My father's visiting friends in France,' Raymond had told her as they had parted the evening before, 'and, as you already know, my brother's away on business. Tomorrow I come down to earth,' he had added reluctantly, 'and go back to my job in the town.'

He had already told her that he was employed as a junior accountant in the office from which the Hotel Panorama Grand was run.

'It's OK,' she had reassured him, 'I'm sure I'll find plenty to do.'

Now she gave her attention to the sweeping panorama — after which the hotel was no doubt named — which stretched as far to the left and right as she could crane her neck to see. Not a single ripple disturbed the lake's surface. The aroma of coffee from someone else's balcony breakfast brought her out of her reverie just as the town's clock struck a melodious ten.

She re-entered her room, making for the long table on which the hotel's information brochure had been placed. She read,

Switzerland is one of the most multi-lingual countries in Europe. Many Swiss speak several languages. Also, it's a shopper's paradise. Look out for watches, textiles and embroideries, antiques and ski clothes. French, German and Italian gastronomic influences prevail, and each region has its own specialities. And always ask for the local Swiss wines, which are best when young.

Sighing, she closed the stiff-covered folder. If only she possessed sufficient spending money to follow the brochure's advice. But, she reasoned, it didn't stop her from window-shopping, did it?

Taking the lift to the entrance foyer, she deposited her key at Reception. Pushing through a swing-door, she pressed the call button to summon the glass-enclosed funicular which for many years had carried guests to and from the lower level of the lakeside.

The funicular arrived and the door slid open. She stepped in and enjoyed the sensation of descending diagonally to the street, watching the various levels of the hotel pass by.

Crossing the road, she stood for a few moments taking in the view. The lake shone in the bright sunshine that had dissolved the morning's haze. Beyond it distant mountains rose, a majestic backdrop, residual snow capping some of their summits.

Small lake-craft chased each other as a ferry cut a curving line across to its daytime mooring, ready for the day's business. At intervals, ships' hooters rang out, sometimes tunefully mournful, sometimes anxiously hastening other boats out of their way.

The pace of life all around her swept her along, the trees lining the pavement rustling busily in the morning breeze. There were the traffic sounds, trolley-buses passing, the lap of the lake against the shoreline, its waves created by passing boats. Across the road illuminated signs over jewellers' shops advertised famous names: Rolex and Piaget, Avia and Longines, all clutching at your attention, she reflected, making you want to dash across and buy the gold watches, the clocks, the sparkling jewellery displayed beside them. . .provided, of course, that you had the money to spend, which she didn't. Not that kind of money, anyway.

Everything interested her, even the posters on notice-boards advertising the music festival that was to take place soon at the town's concert hall.

The day had passed in a kind of dream. She had lunched and drunk coffee and fruit juice at the open-air cafés which seemed to be everywhere.

She had window-shopped, too, admiring the linens and fine embroidered handkerchiefs so tastefully displayed, loving the patterns and bright colours of the knitted goods, and gazing at the famous Swiss Army knives with their multiplicity of blades.

She had wandered around department stores and stared longingly at the attractive merchandise. The small shops had intrigued her, too. She had loved the cuckoo-clocks displayed around the walls, which clamoured humorously and harmoniously for attention at frequent intervals.

Music boxes had played pleasant tunes as she had idly lifted the lids. She had envisaged the hand-crafted wood carvings and ceramics adorning the built-in shelves of her flat, then remembered with a regretful shock that those shelves did not belong to her any more.

In a dream, she wandered back along the lakeshore, watching the craft, admiring the gold path of the sun on the rippling water.

Opposite the entrance to the funicular and across the road from it she stepped off the kerb, remembering too late that the traffic drove on the opposite side of the road from her own country. The impact of the car was on her left arm and shoulder as they swung with her body; then the road came up and hit her. She heard a ringing scream that filled her ears, and did not realise that it had come from her own throat.

The screech of brakes echoed back and forward in her head as she lay half on, half off the pavement. She realised dimly that she must have lost consciousness for a few moments, because the next thing she knew was that she was lying helpless in a man's arms.

CHAPTER TWO

ABIGAIL'S eyes fluttered open and she felt her dry lips move. 'Raymond?' she heard herself whisper, then became aware that something about the word sounded wrong. 'How did you. . .?' Her eyes locked with those above, and the world started to spin slowly and relentlessly around her.

Raymond's blue eyes were there, and Raymond's nose and mouth, but the thrusting jaw and compressed lips were not his. Nor was the strange and haunting scent of the stranger in the least like Raymond's. But she had surely seen this man before?

Sounds intruded. There were questions in German, angry voices raised, arguments going back and forth over her tired head.

'*Krankenhaus*?'

Why did something tell her that the word meant hospital? She had seen it in the hotel's folder. 'No, no hospital,' she heard herself plead. 'I'm OK, I'm——'

She was being lowered to the ground. Hands started moving over her, thoroughly, clinically searching, and for some reason that was beyond her she discovered that she did not object at all to their touch.

'No broken bones, I am convinced,' said someone in English, no doubt so that she would understand. 'Shock, probably, and some concussion, maybe. I will take responsibility for this young lady. I will call a doctor. *Mein Gott*, it was I who hit her, was it not? And no, Miss Hailey,' he said through gritted teeth, 'it is *not* Raymond.'

The angry declaration was spoken by a voice she could swear she had heard before. 'And hospital will not be necessary.' Which meant that she had guessed right.

Her body was swung through the air and placed full-length with unbelievable gentleness, and in complete contrast to the tone of voice, on the rear seat of a car.

There was a police siren, the slamming of doors, then the whole population of the town seemed to be gazing in at her. '*Doktor*' was mentioned, and the word '*nein*', repeated in the voice that was growing increasingly and disturbingly familiar.

'*Ja, ein Unglücksfall*, an accident.' There followed a long interchange between the man and the police. Abigail heard a sighing cry, only to realise that it had come from her own lungs, her own lips. She felt so tired. If sleep was a way of escaping from the pain, then she would sleep. . .

It seemed to be hours later that she found herself in bed. 'No concussion,' someone was saying. 'Shock, bruising. . .' There followed a conversation in German, the voice of one of the participants being worryingly familiar.

A door closed and she thought she was alone, but another voice — Raymond's — exclaimed, 'For God's sake, Rolf, how could you have done such a thing? If she dies, or if she's injured for life, I'll —— '

'Calm down, Brother. And cut out the drama. Shock, the doctor said, cuts and bruises, which have received attention. She'll ache like hell for two or three days, then she should be back to normal. Now, Miss Hailey, I believe you are awake?'

Her eyes came open and that face was there again, Raymond's yet not Raymond's, eyes more piercing, gaze more penetrating, the sweep of the jaw to a rounded chin giving a resolution and determination that Raymond's would never possess. The lower lip was full, the upper well shaped, the two combining to give an impression of a man accustomed to giving orders and expecting them to be obeyed.

'Ah, you are receiving me,' Rolf said. 'So tell me, Miss Hailey, whose fault was it that the accident occurred?'

'Stop pressurising her and stop interrogating her,'

Raymond exclaimed. 'If she answers in the way you want, it would be under duress.'

'*Duress*?'

Under his brother's incredulous stare, Raymond rephrased a little hesitantly, 'What I mean is, in her present state she's reliant on the Felder family's generosity, especially yours, for her immediate welfare. You knocked her down, but it goes without saying, doesn't it, that she won't blame *you*?'

'It *was* my fault, Raymond,' Abigail interposed, her voice tremulous with shock. 'I was in a foreign country; I was in a—a kind of dream. I just forgot which side the traffic drove. . .stepped off the pavement. . .'

'There,' Raymond exclaimed with some bitterness, 'you have your confession now. You are exonerated, dear brother. And shouldn't you have recorded it, to be played back as evidence of your innocence at any court proceedings she might bring against you?'

'Oh, please, Raymond.' Abigail felt that she had to come to the aid of the man who had, through no fault of his own, sent her flying. 'It was not your brother who caused the accident. It was stupid of me to forget. . .' Her voice trailed away and she felt tears slipping down her cheeks. They surprised her; she didn't know why they were there.

'There is no need, Miss Hailey, to act the lawyer on my behalf,' came the gruff voice of the elder brother. 'There are plenty of witnesses who would be willing to testify in my favour.'

'I'm taking the blame, Mr Felder,' she heard herself cry, then a sob took her by surprise and she turned her head against the pillow, only to wince at the pain the action caused.

'Abigail!' Raymond was leaning over her. 'Don't cry, Abby. Look, I'll stay off work this afternoon and——'

'You want me to pull rank, Raymond?' Rolf interjected through his teeth. He glanced at his watch. 'You're late as it is.'

'One day——' Raymond turned on his brother, fist raised, then made for the door '—I'll. . .'

Rolf's head jerked towards the corridor. Get the hell out, the action said. The door closed with a crash.

Rolf's hand made for a pocket and a fresh-smelling square of cotton gently absorbed Abigail's tears. Try as she might to stop them, they just kept coming. With a smothered exclamation, Rolf sat on the bed beside her, smoothing her brow and stroking errant strands of hair away from her damp skin.

'Abigail?' His voice was strangely husky, his hard gaze undergoing a sea change and softening inexplicably as he looked down at her. 'It is the shock emerging.'

Surprise at his use of her first name stopped her in mid-sob, but a shudder of a sigh overtook her. An arm slid beneath her and she felt her limp form being gathered up and pulled against him. There was a scent about him, she noticed again, that bore no resemblance to that of Raymond. It was fresh, yet musky; it was like a magnet to her sense of smell. She wanted to bury her face in its powerful masculinity and never be parted from it again.

Her sobs, she noticed abstractedly, had stopped. She didn't feel the need to cry any more because, an insistent voice inside her said, she had come home, hadn't she? She had come in from the emotional cold.

Her head lifted and their eyes enmeshed, hers holding a query, his the answer. Slowly, almost imperceptibly, his head lowered and his mouth made fleeting contact with hers. But that, it seemed, had been intended as only a preliminary gesture. What followed was heady and intoxicating, his lips playing with hers until, helplessly, she allowed him access. Then it was over and her breathing was deep and painful.

Oh, no, her rational side reproached her, this man's body was no safe harbour. He had this dislike of women—hadn't Raymond warned her?—regarding them merely as playthings, to be used and discarded if the words 'commitment' and 'permanency' ever drifted into their vocabulary.

Averting her eyes, she struggled to move away, and he lowered her back on to the pillows.

'What's wrong, Miss Hailey?' came from his lips sharply. So, despite the momentary intimacy of their kiss, they were back to formality. She had been warned, hadn't she? 'In the good old-fashioned way, I tried to "kiss it better". But it didn't work, hmm?'

'It's made it worse,' she gasped, genuinely in distress from her injuries now.

He uttered some words under his breath, but they were in his own language. 'Then I am sorry,' he averred, his tone strangely softened, 'but your eyes kissed mine before my lips touched yours. In other words——'

'I didn't ask for that kiss, I did not!' she protested agitatedly.

'Be honest, then, and admit that it was the wrong man who kissed you.'

No! But, an inner voice dictated, admit it, if only to yourself, that it was the *right* man. . .

'The wrong man, yes,' she heard her own unbelievably steady voice answer. 'Now will—will you please go?'

When he rose, she thought he was about to obey her faltering command. Instead, he walked to the window, halfway to the door, then turned to the full-length mirror on the wall.

'I shall provide you with a nurse, and any other medical personnel you might require to help your recovery.'

She saw with a shock that he was monitoring not his own reflection, but her reactions through the mirror.

'Thank you, but——' she drew in a shaky breath '—there's no need to—to flaunt your wealth in front of me.' She heard the quick snap of his teeth, but went on, risking his anger. 'Raymond told me your opinion of women: that all they want is money and position, and that they place love very low on their scale of values. Well, I'm different, Mr Felder. Top of *my* list of a man's desirable characteristics is honesty and integrity and—and compassion. Most important, warmth of heart and tenderness and — and the capacity to love.'

'You're looking for a paragon, Miss Hailey.' His lips twisted. 'You will not find him, except in your dreams.'

His eyes had not moved from her reflection, nor had his rigid position altered. His hands stayed in his pockets; his face hadn't lost an atom of its coldness.

She shrugged against the pillows, then frowned at the resulting pain. 'If I have to go through life alone,' she burst out, 'it would be better than being tied to a man who disliked women so much that he used them and discarded them — a man like you!'

'You know everything about me, do you?' came from him darkly.

The moment the accusing words had left her lips she regretted them, but something drove her on.

'From what Raymond told me about you,' she went on recklessly, 'it's probably only a matter of time before you start blaming me for initiating the accident — throwing myself in front of your car, for instance — so as to take legal action against you, and in that way to get a lot of money out of you for the injuries you caused.'

'Your opinion of me is of no consequence.' His jaw moved, his eyes narrowed, and he turned to face her. 'For my brother's sake, I shall take all the care of you that is necessary. Even if, Miss Hailey——' he approached the bed, a touch of menace in his expression '— you do try my patience to its limits.'

He looked down at her and for no explicable reason a shiver took hold. 'Sh-shock,' she got out, tensing in case he touched her again. 'Th-the accident.'

It might have been shock, she admitted to herself, but there was no doubt about it: mixed in was the impact on her sensibilities of his electric presence, his thick brows drawn together, the set of his mouth that had so recently taken possession of hers.

'So,' he said softly, 'it's compensation you're after, after all.'

'Stop insulting me,' she cried. 'I wouldn't touch a single piece of your money.'

'No?' His lip lifted contemptuously. 'We shall see, will we not?' The door hammered home behind him.

Three days later Abigail was recovered enough to sit on the balcony for breakfast.

Rolf had kept his word. He had provided a nurse, a smiling, softly spoken lady who told Abigail that she was employed by Herr Felder in the role of hotel nurse, rotating in her duties with two others. Doctors were on call to attend at the hotel whenever extra medical help was needed, and it had been one of these who had examined Abigail on the day of the accident.

'I believe you slept through most of it,' the nurse, called Vera, confided. She had attended to Abigail's cuts and grazes, gently bathing the bruises and generally making her comfortable.

Raymond had called on her every day, staying as long as she had felt able to tolerate his high spirits. On one occasion Rolf had joined him.

'You see, Miss Hailey,' he had said, eyes sardonic, 'that I did not have to "flaunt my wealth in front of you" by hiring a nurse. She is a member of the hotel staff.'

Abigail coloured deeply as Raymond stared. 'Nurse Vera did tell me. Thank you for that. And I'm sorry for——'

'She said that?' Raymond exclaimed on a note of laughter, a finger indicating Abigail.

'She said more, much more,' came the laconic reply. 'My skin is still grazed where she scratched me with her claws.'

Raymond took Abigail's hand and inspected it. 'Claws? She doesn't have any.'

His brother's eyebrows lifted sardonically, but he made no comment. Instead, he watched them together, his face unreadable as Raymond, seated on the arm of Abigail's chair, talked and joked and made her laugh. His arm had strayed around her shoulders and Abigail had tensed just a little, knowing—and knowing that Raymond knew—that there was in reality nothing serious between them. Yet there he sat, doing his best to give his brother the impression that there was.

When Raymond lifted her hand to his lips in an extravagantly affectionate gesture she retrieved it with an unintentional jerk of the arm. The cynicism in the elder brother's eyes made her curl up inside. He was, she was sure, recalling her outburst about her list of requirements in a man, denying his contention that all women wanted in life was money and position.

Wasn't she at that moment, that brother's expression was saying, encouraging the attentions of a young man with the power and the money of his family behind him, not to mention the executive and well-paid position that would surely be his one day in the future?

It was on her first day up and dressed that she heard laughter in the corridor and Raymond's voice saying, 'This room. It's OK, we just go in.' The door swung wide. 'Don't we, Abby?'

'Raymond!' Abigail exclaimed. 'It's a good thing I was decent——'

'Hi.' A female version of Raymond erupted into the room. 'I am Martina Felder. You are Abigail Hailey. I was so sorry to hear that my ogre of a big brother sent you flying. What a welcome to the country of the Felders!'

Abigail smiled, then stared.

'It's OK,' Martina commented, 'I know you think you are seeing double, but Raymond and I are twins. Did he forget to tell you? We have a fond-fight relationship.'

'Mostly fight,' mumbled Raymond, pushing away the female fist that kept threatening his chin.

'I hope you are feeling better,' Martina addressed Abigail. 'Your colour is good. Or is it that Raymond has come to see you? He said that you're his girl.'

'Did he? Well, I. . .'

'He's assuming too much? You like him a lot, but. . .' Martina nodded. 'I understand. I have boyfriends, too.

In the plural. It's safer. They're OK.' She smiled. 'Raymond, you'll have to try harder to win your guest's affection. Or maybe——' Martina studied Abigail '—there's someone else?'

Abigail frowned. There is, she wanted to say, but for heaven's sake who? For the life of her, she couldn't put a name to him. 'There was,' she answered at last, 'but he——' she shrugged '—he liked another girl better.'

'Idiot,' snorted Martina's twin.

'Raymond told me you're in the fashion business,' Abigail remarked, having taken an immediate liking to Raymond's twin sister.

Martina nodded. 'I design and create clothes. I design fabrics, too. I have a workshop in the hotel basement. When I left college I started a business. It's called Martina Models.' She made a face. 'Not very original, but people seem to remember it. Anyway, my father backed me financially in setting it up and now I employ people to help me. I don't go in for mass production. Often my workshop produces one-offs—that is, designs created solely for ladies who don't need to count the pennies, as the saying is in your country.'

Abigail nodded.

'My other designs aren't exactly cheap, either, but on the other hand they don't break a working girl's bank balance. Some of my efforts are on display in the windows of the fashion shop in the hotel entrance.'

'Those are yours?' Abigail exclaimed. 'They're just great.'

'She's flattering you, Martina,' Raymond commented. 'She's wanting you to design something especially for her.'

'No, I'm not.' Abigail stared at him, and he pretended to shrivel under her fierce regard. 'You're talking just like your brother, implying that I'm merely a gold-digger, out for what I can get from a man. Or, in this case, Martina.'

The door opened.

'Talk of the devil,' Raymond declared, grinning at Rolf, 'and he comes. Join the party.'

Rolf's eyes swung round the semicircle, settling at last on Abigail's seated figure. His eyes plainly missed nothing, neither her bright eyes, nor her flushed and smiling face.

'My siblings appear to be good medicine, Miss Hailey. Unlike the Felder family's first-born.'

'Meaning you, Mr Felder? I'm sorry — *Herr* Felder.'

'What is all this——' Martina gestured '—all this formality? She and I have only just met, yet we're on first-name terms. For goodness' sake, Abigail, call him Rolf. And you, Rolf——'

'If I were to address her informally,' came Rolf's dry reply, 'she might accuse me of trying to ingratiate myself with her in order to persuade her not to take me to court for knocking her down.'

The twins laughed.

'Just before you staged your entrance,' Raymond remarked, 'she was accusing me of being just like you. In a derogatory sense, she meant.'

'In our short acquaintance——' Rolf's hooded eyes noted Abigail's flushed confusion '—I cannot recall her referring to me in anything but derogatory terms.'

'You as good as accused me,' Abigail rounded on him, 'of being the sort who treats a man merely as a source of material gain.'

'He did?' Raymond placed a protective arm around her shoulders. 'It's my girlfriend you're insulting.'

'She's your girlfriend?' Martina queried. 'Since when?'

I have to clear this matter up once and for all, Abigail thought. 'Not true,' she declared, her smile a little strained as she glanced up at Raymond. 'We're friends, great friends, but. . .' She shook her head at Raymond's down-turned mouth. 'It's true, Raymond, you have to admit it; no more than friends.'

'I'd wait, I said.'

'That'll have to be for a long time, it seems,' his sister interposed in her down-to-earth fashion. 'The lady means it.'

Strike now, an inner voice advised Abigail. 'Which is why I can't go on accepting Raymond's hospitality.'

'She means she wants to sing for her supper,' remarked Martina. She turned to her elder brother. 'She wants to work her passage. She wants a job. Right, Abigail?'

Abigail nodded, looking under her lashes for Rolf's reaction. He saw her glance and his eyes grew hooded, speculative, as if assessing her sensual attributes. Oh, no, she thought, he's misinterpreting. He thinks I'm offering — well, what I'm certainly not offering.

'OK, Rolf,' Raymond sighed. 'So Abigail and I did discuss some possible jobs she might tackle. For instance — ' he counted on his fingers ' — working behind the bar. Assistant in the kitchens. Serving at tables — '

Rolf swung to face her. 'You have experience in all these things?'

He's interviewing me, Abigail thought, heart sinking at his seeming lack of sympathy for her cause.

'Not really. But I'd be more than willing to learn. I'm a reasonable cook. I know how to wash dishes.'

'We've been to bars together,' Raymond offered helpfully, 'and experimented with different tastes.'

Rolf folded his arms and placed his feet a little apart, firming his stance and presenting an alarmingly authoritative figure to Abigail's now less than hopeful gaze.

'One, we employ only highly experienced staff in the kitchens,' he declared crisply. 'The chefs would not tolerate an absolute beginner, nor would the hotel management. Two, all our staff are trained in their respective trades and skills, with certificates or diplomas to prove it.'

When would he stop putting her down? Abigail wondered, heart sinking.

'Three,' he persisted relentlessly, 'we have mechanical means of washing dishes. Four, the assistants in the hotel's various bars are highly experienced, as are the waiting staff, not to mention the chamber-maids.'

'So ——' why did her voice have to sound so tremulous? ' — no job vacancies.'

'No job vacancies, sorry.'

To Abigail, he sounded anything but sorry.

'Can't you be more sympathetic?' his sister asked. 'After all, it doesn't matter whose fault it was; it remains a fact that you, in your car, knocked her down and injured her.'

His mouth firmed; his eyes hardened. 'It seems, Miss Hailey, that you have half of my family on your side. However, together with my father, I run this hotel chain ——'

'And with you against me, I might as well pack up and go.' Why did her voice have to wobble so?

'Will you leave her alone?' said Raymond, putting a protective arm around her. She winced a little; she couldn't help it.

'You are still in pain, Miss Hailey?'

The man saw too much, Abigail thought. 'It's the shoulder which you — which your car. . .'

'You see,' Martina put in, 'she's still too nice, too polite to accuse you outright of sending her flying.'

'It was she who stepped into my path,' he corrected his sister, 'not I who deliberately drove my car at her.'

His words revived the memory of the impact, and she felt her cheeks drain.

'For heaven's sake, Rolf. . .' Raymond stroked her hair. 'She's still suffering from shock, can't you see?'

'No, I'm not,' Abigail protested. 'It's — it's your brother. . .his attitude; it's so hard and unfeeling.'

The brother to whom she referred turned on his heel. Just before he reached the door, Raymond added, 'That just about sums up his character. So beware, Abigail. Have as few dealings with him as possible.'

The door closed behind Rolf Felder with a quietness that told of an anger determinedly suppressed, and was all the more intimidating for it, Abigail thought restlessly.

* * *

'Have breakfast with me this morning,' Martina's voice came persuasively over the telephone in Abigail's room two days later, 'that is, if you are fit enough.'

'I'm fine now, honestly,' Abigail assured her, 'and yes, I'd love to. It'll be a change from having it here on my own.'

They met at the door of the restaurant and Martina led her to the table she had shared with Raymond before the accident. He was there, and looked round, beaming.

'Here, sit beside me. Now where do we start? Is that what you are wanting to know?'

It was a window table and the lake sparkled in the sunshine. Yachts, bare masts ready and waiting for the sails to be hoisted, floated serenely, admiring their own reflections in the calm water. The distant mountains were hazed and all the more mysterious for it.

'It's a beautiful morning,' Abigail exclaimed.

'There she is,' Raymond remarked, 'feasting her eyes instead of satisfying her inner needs.' As the waiter approached he added, 'What is it to be, Abigail — tea or coffee?'

Abigail chose coffee.

'Now, Abby, since this is the first time you've taken breakfast with the common herd — '

'Thanks to our careless brother knocking her down,' Martina interposed.

'No, no, it was my — '

Raymond ignored Abigail's attempt to put the record straight. 'Our guests,' he pointed out, 'help themselves at this meal. So come, Abby, follow me.'

He led the way to the side-tables, filled with a variety of foods.

Five minutes later they returned with glasses of fruit juice, and plates piled with hunks of dark wholemeal and grain-speckled bread. Martina returned with a dish of fruit, while Raymond came back with a plate of assorted meats. Abigail had her usual breakfast of muesli, fresh fruits, croissants and honey and marmalade.

'*Gipfeli*, we call those.' Raymond pointed to Abigail's croissants. 'We Swiss are particular about our bread. It has to be crusty and crisp. Hand-made, too. It's a matter of pride in our bakeries. So, Abigail——' he reached out to pat her hand '—enjoy, as they say.'

And Abigail proceeded to do so, sinking her white teeth into each delicious-tasting portion.

'You are allowed to go back for more,' he told her.

'Don't encourage her to spoil her figure,' his sister reprimanded. 'It's just about perfect as it is.'

Abigail flushed and shook her head. 'I need to lose——'

'You need to lose nothing,' Martina interrupted. 'There are some models who would envy you your shape.'

Raymond said nothing, but his appreciative gaze spoke volumes. 'All the same,' he declared, 'one day Martina and I must take you to a *Konditorei*, *pâtisserie*, or *pasticceria*—that is, one of the tearooms in the town—and buy you one of the luscious creations they sell—pastries, as I think you call them, with honey and almonds and with cream and chocolate spilling out as you sink your teeth into them.'

'You're making Abigail's mouth water, Raymond. Will you stop it? Or she will go home with more weight than she arrived with.'

Raymond scrunched his pure white table napkin into creases. 'Did you know,' he said, 'that we German-speaking Swiss call the potato the *Erdöpfel*, the earth apple? And that we do wonderful things with it? And that when, nearly a hundred years ago, a man called Dr Bircher-Benner opened a private clinic in Zurich he liked the nutritional value of the *orchard* apple so much that he added the whole fruit, grated, with the core, pips and skin, along with nuts and berries, to milk? Which was—can you guess?—how the now famous Swiss muesli was invented.'

'And which I've just had with my breakfast.'

'Right,' commented Martina, with some pride.

'Today it's a Swiss national dish and served all over this country. More coffee, Abigail? Do help yourself.'

Gallantly Raymond poured the coffee for her, then glanced at his watch. He sprang to his feet. 'Please excuse me. If I'm late for work, my dear brother will tear me into little strips, as they say. See you later, yes, Abigail?'

'He's always late for work,' Martina remarked, watching him weaving fast between tables. 'Now my work today is taking me into the town. Would you like to come with me, Abigail? Would you feel fit enough?'

Abigail assured her that she would. 'I went on a walkabout my first day here, before I——'

'Before my dear elder brother drove his car into you,' she broke in. 'He owes you for that, Abigail.'

'I owe her for what?'

Abigail nearly jumped out of her skin as the man about whom they were talking appeared at her side.

'Knocking her over, injuring her.'

'Is that what you think, Miss Hailey?'

'You know my thoughts on that subject,' Abigail returned, wishing she did not flush so easily.

'She's coming with me today,' Martina told him, folding her table napkin carefully, unlike her brother. She stood up. 'She's fit enough, she said.'

Abigail rose, too, her left shoulder coming into contact with Rolf's broad chest, and she could not stop herself from flinching.

'You're still in pain?' he queried. 'I could request the services of a physiotherapist, if you think that would ease it.'

She could not tell him that he was partly the cause of her wincing. Any contact with his powerful physique, she had discovered, caused electric currents to sting her right where her body had touched his.

'Thanks, but no,' she answered. 'I'll wait for nature to do its stuff and repair the damage.'

His shrug told her, As you wish. To Martina he said, 'There's been a phone call from Father. He's moved from the States to Canada. He's fine.' Martina's smile told him how pleased she was. 'I shall be in Zurich today,' he told her, then turned to Abigail. 'You will be safe — relatively —' with a faintly derogatory smile at his sister ' — in Martina's hands.' He turned to go.

'Herr Felder.' Abigail's voice halted him. He half turned. 'I'm still determined to pay my way while I'm here. Or, alternatively, insist that I'm given a job.'

'I shall give the matter my undivided and most meticulous attention,' was his mocking comment. 'But I have to admit, Miss Hailey, that it's not exactly high on my list of priorities.' With which sardonic comment, he went on his way.

CHAPTER THREE

MARTINA whisked Abigail downtown in her little car.

'First,' she said, 'we go to Gisela's, where I have business to conduct.'

She swept into a small, select boutique where, in Abigail's eyes, the price of the clothes on display seemed to be beyond her ability to pay. Maybe in Switzerland, she reflected, the 'working-girls' to whom Martina had referred earned more than their equivalent where she came from.

The lady assistant welcomed Martina warmly and invited Abigail to look around while they were busy. They disappeared into a back-room, and another assistant approached Abigail.

'*Guten Tag*,' the lady said, '*Bitte schön*?'

At least I can make an enquiry, Abigail thought. She gestured towards the shop window. 'That dress. . .'

To Abigail's relief, the assistant switched instantly to English. 'It is beautiful, madam,' she said, expertly assessing Abigail's measurements, 'and I'm sure it would fit you. The colour, also, with your dark hair. . .' She was moving towards the window.

'But how much. . .? I mean the cost. . .?'

'You wish me to tell you in English pounds?' She used a pocket calculator and told Abigail the answer. At which Abigail stifled a gasp and shook her head.

'I couldn't afford that. Thank you, but. . .' Her gaze lingered on the dress. It was so right for her!

The assistant, quick to seize on Abigail's hesitation, said, 'I will get it from the window.'

Abigail waited, thinking, What harm would there be in trying it on?

'Yes, it fits perfectly, madam,' the assistant encouraged, and Abigail agreed, but reluctantly shook her head.

'Please,' the assistant said. 'You are a visitor?'

'Yes, but it's no use. I couldn't possibly——'

'Couldn't possibly what?' asked Martina, reappearing and summing up the situation instantly. 'That dress? Yes, it's you. It's also one of my creations. You must have it.'

'No!' Abigail smiled to tone down her refusal. 'Not without——'

'Please, Abby, forget the cost. My brother will pay. He owes you; he owes you so much. After all, look what he did, causing you so much pain and discomfort. I will have the bill sent to him. The matter is settled.'

She made arrangements with the assistant, unheeding of Abigail's agitated, 'You really mustn't.'

'Come,' she said when Abigail had changed back into her own clothes. 'I will give you a whirlwind tour of the town.'

Having arranged for the dress to be delivered to the hotel that afternoon, Martina whisked Abigail through the city's streets.

She showed Abigail the city's cobbled squares rustling with trees, the half-hidden courtyards, the huge frescoes painted on the external walls of houses and public buildings. They depicted in semi-caricature people of olden times seated at table, a mother holding a tiny offspring. There were fun figures, too: 'flying' clowns blowing horns, and paintings, fanciful and sometimes strange, of creatures from the artists' imagination.

Along narrow paved areas were department stores and smaller shops, shaded by tall buildings and brightened by colourful flags strung across.

'Here is the old city,' Martina said, sweeping Abigail from one picturesque area to another, up long flights of steps and down others. 'See, here under these arches is a giant chess set. And here is a little square with a fountain in the centre, just one of many squares in the town.'

They had lunch at a table by wrought-iron railings beside the river into which the lake flowed. Birds rose and dipped into the water, their feathers now and then falling away and floating on the surface.

Fascinated, Abigail let her eyes rest on the reflections of buildings, moving in the ripples. Small boats lined the banks, while swans drifted graciously among them. Above and around them, in the semi-distance, rose the mountains, ridged by time or forested, like a majestic backdrop.

'Listen,' said Martina, stirring her coffee, 'to all the languages around us. People come here from all over the world.'

She pointed across the street to a chemist's shop. 'An *Apotheke*. It's very ancient, but it's closed now. See the words in German painted over it. I'll translate. "There is no herb against love".' She laughed. 'That is something I have yet to experience. I'm far too busy running my business. You?'

'Have I been in love?' For some curious reason, Abigail found it hard to reply. 'Not until. . .' What am I saying? she chided herself. 'Not really,' she amended, but something inside her began to wish that there did exist a herb, or something, which would guard against her loving the wrong person. But who was this 'wrong person'? It was a question whose answer filled her with a curious sort of apprehension.

Martina seemed, to Abigail's relief, contented with her answer.

They walked back to the car through another cobbled square — mid-sixteenth-century, Martina explained — below balconies bedecked with bright flowers and beneath flags displayed with pride from upstairs windows.

'Your dress should have been delivered by now,' Martina remarked, as they ascended in the funicular to the hotel entrance. 'I requested that it should be taken to my workroom so that I can decide if any alterations need to be made. I hope you don't mind.'

Abigail laughed, shaking her head. She had the notion that even if she had objected it would have been determinedly overruled.

They descended by lift and Martina beckoned to Abigail to follow her as she thrust open a door and walked in.

'Please forgive the chaos,' Martina remarked, gesturing, 'because that is what this is. It's how a creative artist. . .well——' with a smile '—creates. That's my excuse, anyway.'

Abigail had a vague impression of clothes and fabrics everywhere, draped from above like curtains, or across tables and chairs, or on hangers hooked on the backs of doors. There were sewing machines and needlework accessories strewn over trestle-tables, on footstools and even on windowsills.

'No production lines here,' Martina said with some pride. 'No factory atmosphere. I'm just a small business operating, quite successfully, actually, for the benefit of ladies who like to look different. Over there——' her arm waved vaguely towards a long rail of garments totally hidden by a giant piece of cloth '—are my designs waiting for a fashion show.'

Removing her jacket, she invited Abigail to dispense with hers.

'It's to be staged in the grounds of the house that's being renovated for us—Raymond told you? Not long now, then we can get back to a normal domestic way of life. I shall move my business to a room which I've specially chosen there for its good light. There'll be a party—a grand one—to celebrate the finish of the renovations and the Felder family's move into the house.'

'Hi,' she said to a blonde-haired young woman standing at an ironing-board, meticulously pressing a jacket. 'This is Abigail Hailey, a friend of mine and Raymond's, too. She's British. Abigail, this is Liliane Schmidt.' The young woman met Abigail's smile with her own. 'Has a dress been delivered from Gisela's?' Martina enquired.

Abigail recognised the name as belonging to the shop in the town which she and Martina had visited.

'It has,' Liliane answered, following Martina's example and speaking in English. 'It is over there.'

Even though it was just draped on a clothes hanger on the door, the colours in the dress sang out, the bold splashes and lines adding light to the air around it.

'I'm sure,' the assistant added, 'that it's one of yours, Martina.'

'It is. For a newcomer to my workshop,' Martina returned, 'it is very observant of you to notice. Now, Abigail, we will try it on, yes?'

Abigail glanced around, frowning. 'Here?'

'Why not? No one — by that I mean no male — will come in. And there's a changing-cubicle with a mirror if you insist on being shy.'

Abigail retreated into this, changing into the dress but first pulling the curtain across. Martina tutted and opened it again and it was as she knelt, adjusting the hem, that there came a tap at the door and Raymond entered. 'Friend, not foe trying to steal your ideas,' he joked.

'You said——' Abigail exclaimed to Martina.

'You call *him* a male?' Raymond's twin sister muttered, absorbed in her work. 'I don't.'

'Hi,' said Raymond. 'Hey.' His eyes fastened on Abigail. 'Wow.'

'Are you,' his sister commented, 'commenting on my brilliant design or, more probably, Abigail's figure?'

'More probably,' Raymond replied, with a broad, appreciative grin. He looked around, noticing the new assistant for the first time. It seemed to take him a few moments to take a breath. 'Hi. Er — Martina?' Introduce me, his voice said.

'What? Oh. Liliane, this is my little brother Raymond.'

'Not so much of the little,' Raymond reproached, plainly taken with the young woman's looks. 'Have you worked here long, Liliane?'

'Three weeks,' his sister answered for her, as Liliane seemed too confused to reply.

'Ah.' Raymond nodded, appearing somewhat bemused himself. 'So. I must——'

'You must take the lift upwards,' said his sister.

Raymond grimaced at his sister's novel way of telling him to go, and took the hint. Which, thought Abigail, was just as well, since Martina, having also made some adjustments to the fit of the dress around the waistline, was helping her to divest herself of the garment.

On its way it had covered her head, and through the fabric she had heard vague sounds of Raymond muttering, 'Hi, don't go into the lion's den. They'll bite your head off.'

It was only when she eventually emerged breathless from the folds of the dress that Abigail, finding herself facing the mirror, saw a tall, broad-shouldered man studying her reflection with uninhibited interest. With a shock, she realised that he could see both the front of her and her back, which, since she was wearing the minimum of underwear, made her very embarrassed indeed.

'Martina!' she exclaimed agitatedly. 'Your brother——'

'Don't fret, Abby,' she reproached, totally absorbed in her work. 'Raymond's gone, so relax.'

Relax? Abigail thought, with that hunk of manhood studying her reflection from head to foot in the minutest detail? She swung round. 'Will you please go?' Then she realised what she had done—given him a clear and uncluttered view, not of the reflection, but of the real thing.

'Oh, you mean Rolf,' commented Martina matter-of-factly, glancing up. 'Don't worry about him. He's used to ladies in a state of un——'

'Please,' Abigail begged, hugging herself and wishing her bra and briefs had more substance to them. 'Is there a robe, or something?'

From across the room, Martina looked up at last, scanning her brother's face. 'Well. Yes. I see the animal hunger in that male creature's physiognomy. So——' she pointed to a silk robe draped across a stool '—Liliane be a dear and give that to my friend.'

Rolf was there first. 'I'll save Liliane the trouble.' He carried the garment towards Abigail like, she thought, a tiger about to capture its prey. Her hand reached out, but he ignored it.

'Allow me, Miss Hailey.' He opened it, deliberately

keeping her waiting for a few tantalising moments, taking full advantage of his close proximity to the object of his mocking attention.

'Will you give it to me?' she exclaimed, eyes burning with indignation under his scrutiny. Her hand jerked towards it, but he held it away, his smile taut. She took a deep breath and whispered, 'Please, Herr Felder.'

'Rolf,' he prompted softly.

'Rolf.'

'Stop annoying my customer,' Martina said through the pins held dangerously between her teeth. 'After all, she's our guest.'

At last he relented, going behind Abigail and holding it around her shoulders. His knuckles made her flesh jump, bringing it alarmingly alive, his breath stirred her hair, and his lips, she was certain, brushed against her shoulder just before he helped her to slip her arms into the sleeves.

A shiver took hold, caused not by a feeling of chill, but by his electric nearness. She recalled the pressure of his lips on her mouth the day he had kissed her, and now they trembled minutely of their own accord.

For heaven's sake, she reprimanded her wayward reflexes, was she wanting him to kiss her *again*? He's only Raymond's and Martina's brother, isn't he? And not even as pleasant and friendly as they are.

But, the femininity in her argued, he's more, much more, than ever Raymond is or ever could be, more, even, than Des Casey was. More attractive, more irresistible, more desirable, in fact, than any man she had ever met before.

When he moved away she felt her tension decrease, leaving her as limp and deprived of breath as if she had run up a down-moving escalator.

'You know very well,' scolded his sister, attention only partly on the person she was addressing, 'that all males are banned from this area.'

So, Abigail noted, holding the robe tightly around her, Martina regards *this* brother as male. And who could deny his essential masculinity? she thought. It

was there in force, from the top of his dark head of hair
to his well-shod feet. No wonder the lady called Laura,
the financial journalist whose photograph she had seen
in his room, had chosen him, of all the men with whom
her work must have brought her into contact, to be
her — her what? Partner? Lover? *And had he chosen
her*? The question came out of the blue, tormenting
and, yes, painful too.

'Abigail.'

'Yes?'

His eyes held hers. 'I would like to talk to you.'

Why did her heart have to sink like a stone? Because,
by his expressionless face, she was sure that he was
going to tell her that a job could not be found for her.

'Later,' he added, asking Martina, 'How long will
you be keeping your *customer* here?'

'For as long as it takes her to dress. And, for your
information ——' she glanced up, a gleam of mischief in
her eyes '— you may not know it, but *you* are my
customer.'

The thickly marked eyebrows lifted in query.

'I'm sending you the bill for this dress, big brother,
and it won't be cheap. You owe her for knocking her
down; in fact you owe her a lot. You had a good view
just now, didn't you, of the result of the injuries your
car — you — inflicted?'

In some surprise, Abigail looked down at herself.
She had forgotten about the gradually healing grazes,
the bruises which lingered still, their colours startling
against the whiteness of her skin.

'I told you,' she reproached Martina, 'that your
brother owes me nothing. I was the one who ——'

'He's got brakes, hasn't he? And there's nothing
wrong with his reflexes. Why didn't he stop in time?'

'Martina,' Rolf said on a long-suffering sigh, 'even
for a sister you are being unbelievably obtuse. When a
driver doesn't even see the object that puts itself in his
path he has every right to assume that the road in front
of him is clear of obstacles. However ——' with a
lightning up-and-down glance at the person about

whom they were talking '—I am more than willing to
foot the bill. I assume that the lady in question looks as
good wearing it as she does when she is *not* wearing it.
Fifteen minutes, Abigail?'

'Phew,' exclaimed Martina, when he had gone, 'my
elder brother can throw his weight about when he
likes.' She laughed. 'In more ways than one, I think,
judging by the satisfied-looking lady called Laura whom
I've seen him around with!'

Abigail just made it, but, even so, Rolf was frowning at
his watch. As she emerged from the lift the frown was
replaced by a half-smile that taunted more than express-
ing pleasure.

'I'm sorry,' Abigail was stung to reply, 'if I'm late for
the interview.'

'You are dead on time,' he responded. 'No, let me
correct that. You are very much alive. I have not
stopped thanking God for that since the day I. . .' He
stopped abruptly. 'Will you follow me, please?'

By his brisk tone, Abigail knew he meant business.
And this was the kind of man, she was convinced, who
never mixed that 'business' with sentiment. Mentally
packing her bags, she waited, hands clasped to steady
them, as he closed the door and walked across to a desk
set at an angle to the room.

It was then that she realised that the room was an
office, containing a couple of other desks, on one of
which stood a computer and, beside it, a printer.

Yes, she thought, a suitable venue in which to tell
someone they were not wanted.

'Please. . .' He indicated an upright chair. 'You look
as if you were first in line for the executioner.'

The smile he gave almost knocked her off balance,
so transforming was it. From out of the businessman,
in his business suit, came an informal, relaxed human
being. She found herself smiling in response.

'That is better, much better.' He waited until she was
seated, then dropped into the office chair behind
the desk.

She was glad that he couldn't hear the hammering of her heart, nor see the swift excitement that sped around her system at the sudden transition from tycoon to — to what? she asked herself agitatedly. To a handsome, virile, incredibly attractive man? So what if he was? In a few hours — maybe this evening — she would be on her way to the airport, flying home.

'This insistence of yours to work your passage.' He picked up a letter opener, testing its sharpness.

So he was not going to send her packing after all? Her heart began to rise from the depths to which it had sunk.

Emphatically she nodded.

He tutted. 'It is foolish in the extreme. But ——' his raised hand stopped her protest '— there is a job you can do for me.'

She let out a breath she did not even realise she was holding.

'Or rather, for my father. He has recently retired from the running of the Felder Hotel Group — yes, we own others in this country — as a consequence of which he has passed the chairmanship, with the agreement of the board members, to me. I shall fit in the work alongside the running of my own engineering company in Zurich.'

'You — you need a secretary?'

'Not exactly. There are plenty of those around already.' Dispassionately, he watched the disappointment in her face. 'Another job exists.' A smile flirted with his mouth as her eyes brightened.

He's playing with me, Abigail thought with some annoyance, then cursed her features for revealing so much of what she felt.

'My father has retired from management, but not from work. He is spending his time fulfilling one of his life's ambitions: he's writing a book on the wines of Switzerland. You can type? Good. But are you able to use a computer? You are?' He rose, seeming pleased, inviting her to join him at the desk which held the computer.

'A pile of notes, written in English—he has a British publisher. You think you will be able to understand his scrawl? Here——' his arm across her upper back moved her closer '—have a look.'

At the contact, all her senses had sprung to life, her skin becoming alarmingly sensitised. Her reason put up a fight with her responses, clearing her mind just sufficiently for her to decipher and comprehend the handwriting Rolf was indicating for her comments.

To prove that she understood them, she began reading them aloud. Satisfied, he replaced the notes on the desk, but did not remove his arm.

'The job is yours, Abigail.' He half turned her so that she had to look at him. At that moment she did not care if he read the happiness in her eyes. 'But there are snags.' He watched her face and she could not hide from him the doubt and anxiety his words had produced within her.

'I will explain. It would not please the authorities if you were given a job in this country, together with a salary, without formal permission.'

Abigail nodded, waiting and wondering.

'It might take some time, and in the end you might not be granted the necessary permit.'

Abigail held her breath, this time aware of the fact.

'If you became, as it were, a member of the Felder family——'

'You mean become Raymond's fiancée? I—I couldn't do it, Rolf, not even as a pretence. It wouldn't be fair to him. And I couldn't use him for my own ends. As I said before, I like him a lot, but only as a friend.' Her heart resumed its downward slide.

A small smile tugged at his lips. 'The fiancée, I meant, of the elder Felder brother.'

It took a few moments to register. Her eyes strained upwards, a frown creasing her smooth brow. '*Your* fiancée?' It just wasn't possible, she told herself, so why did her heart have to leap to the heights again? Her sigh was short and from her depths. 'It's no use, Rolf. You have a lady friend; Raymond told me. You know——' she gazed up at him '—you don't have to recompense me in any way for that accident. As I keep saying, it was my——'

His hand came out, his fingers stilling her lips. 'You still bear the bruises. You still have the scars. You. . .'

His voice trailed away. Their eyes, catching fire each from the other, became locked, hers straining upwards, his glancing down. The touch of his hand on her sensitised mouth, the pressure of his palm on her chin, provoked a sensation deep down that tugged at the very heart of her. Then sirens blazed. . . This man is dynamite, they said, his touch explosive; he could at will demolish all your barriers, break down any resistance you might put up. . .and as his 'fiancée', albeit unofficial, anything could happen, couldn't it? Her thoughts chased each other incomprehensibly around her head.

With a shaky hand, she fastened on to his wrist and pulled it away. The contact was broken, but the feelings he had aroused inside her lingered tormentingly.

'A temporary engagement,' he said at last, moving away, his eyes cool now, fire extinguished, with not even a dying ember in sight.

'I would like to think about it,' she said, her voice strangely hoarse. 'Will you give me time?'

'Not long,' was his brisk reply.

'Why—why are you rushing me?'

'Tomorrow morning I shall be interviewing someone for the job from the hotel's office staff.'

Abigail thought, Give him his answer now. Say no, *no*!

'Come, fetch a jacket. While we walk, you will think. Yes?'

Once again, her eyes became ensnared. There was a curious softening of his expression, and she had to tear her gaze from his. In the face of enormous odds, she managed to behave normally, nodding in acquiescence.

'Seven minutes?' she queried, adding with a shaky smile, 'On the dot?'

His eyes smiled too, while his jaw thrust forward at her veiled impudence.

'On the dot as promised,' was his amused comment as she rejoined him in the hotel foyer.

In that seven minutes he had changed. He wore jeans now and had pulled on a dark blouson jacket over an open-necked navy blue shirt from whose unbuttoned neck sprang a shading of dark hair, a piece of very personal information which, Abigail discovered, unaccountably speeded up her pulse-rate. He looked human, she thought, her heart jerking, too human for her own peace of mind.

Raymond emerged from the lift as Rolf took her hand.

'Hey, what. . .?' Raymond demanded. Abigail snatched her hand from Rolf's. 'Aren't you coming to dinner?'

'We have business to discuss,' his elder brother told him. 'And if you dare to say you will join us. . .' He pushed a playful fist in Raymond's direction.

'Remember, Rolf——' there was a worried warning in Raymond's tone '—that it's my girlfriend you're walking off with.'

Abigail shook her head. 'I'm your *friend*, Raymond—a special friend, perhaps, but not—well, the other.'

'So what are you doing,' he asked darkly, gesturing to their now separated hands, 'playing me off against him? Remember, Abby, you're *my* guest.'

'Not any longer,' she answered gently. 'Rolf has offered me a job.' Impatient now, Rolf had thrust his hands into his pockets. Abigail saw the frown and made to join him, saying over her shoulder, 'I'll explain later, Raymond.'

The funicular stood ready and waiting, the door sliding open as the button was pressed. Abigail found herself shut in with Rolf, and once again she felt his proximity overpowering. What if she agreed to his suggestion? How would her femininity—and, more important, her heart—respond to that broad physique, that tensile strength, tightly controlled at the moment, but no doubt devastating when allowed free reign?

As one floor after another flashed past, she told herself that she knew the answer. Hadn't her feelings, her emotions, already become ensnared, no matter how she had tried to untangle them?

He had folded his arms, his legs firmly planted as the funicular bumped a little in its progress to street-level.

'You are thinking, yes?' he asked, looking down at her. A half-smile played with his mouth. 'That is the reason for this silence?'

She nodded, glad beyond words that, although he might read the expressions that passed across her features, he could not read her thoughts.

They walked past the casino, then the moored floating restaurant. At the lakeside, as they were approaching the shopping area, a crowd watched as flocks of pigeons and gulls flew in all directions, like planes lacking radar. People threw scraps, some titbits hitting the waters, others being expertly caught by eager beaks in mid-air.

The birds were so numerous and so eager that it frightened Abigail to find herself in the midst of the swooping, crying creatures, one of which flew within a hand's breadth of her face, seeming to possess an in-built ability to judge the exact distance by which to avoid an object.

She gasped and instinctively swung towards Rolf, who pulled her round and against him, at which action she found her face nestling against his chest.

'Thank you,' she muttered, starting to disentangle herself from his arms. 'Silly of me, but——'

'Reflex action,' he commented with a faint smile. 'Self-preservation.' His broad shoulders shrugged. 'Call it what you like, it was a perfectly natural reaction. It makes a pleasant change,' he added, still holding her shoulders, 'to *rescue* you, rather than being the cause of your trouble.'

'Thanks for the protection, anyway.' She smiled up at him, but his expression on receiving that smile was so serious that Abigail's heart began its downward plunge again. She wished she could read this Felder brother as easily as she read the other.

They found themselves on the city's ancient covered wooden bridge, lifted clear of the water by wooden posts, its tiled roof stretching the whole length, a riot of blooms decorating its parapet.

'The *Kapellbrücke*, circa 1300,' Rolf commented as they stood side by side at the rail. 'It is said to be the world's oldest wooden bridge. The paintings——' he gestured towards the series of overhead panels '—were carried out in the seventeenth and eighteenth centuries. They depict coats of arms of the city's past patrician families, plus local and national events.'

Abigail gazed at them, admiring their colours and artistry.

'Along there, on the bridge, are shops. The water tower——' Rolf indicated the great, stone-built octagonal structure with its cone-shaped roof, its base rising from out of the lake '—was also built about 1300.'

A church bell tolled. For some time there was silence, then she stole a glance at her companion as he gazed at the distant mountains. Her heart turned over at the resolve in his profile, the strength of character it revealed, the brooding look as it dwelt on the rugged peaks, his whole demeanour as remote at that moment as were those summits.

'Yes?' His head turned as if she had spoken, and with narrowed eyes he watched her colour rise. 'You have made up your mind?'

'Yes.' She had to clear her throat. 'Yes, Rolf.' Why did she have to sound so breathless? 'I've decided to accept your offer of a job. . .and the condition that goes with it.'

CHAPTER FOUR

ROLF's response was a brief nod. Why, Abigail asked herself, had her heart sunk without trace? It was, after all, a business arrangement, pure and simple.

'Shall I repeat the terms? No salary attached.' He waited for her nod of agreement. 'Your engagement, unofficial and entirely private, begins as from this moment. I shall make you a monthly allowance. It will be a generous one.'

'But——'

He continued as if she had not spoken. 'An account will be opened for you at my bank. If at any time you discover that your needs are greater than the amount of money deposited in that account, you have only to tell me and I shall increase it. You agree to those terms?'

'Yes.' She was breathless again, as though she had toppled over into the water down there and it was closing over her head.

'Then shall we seal it—with that? No,' he scorned her extended hand, 'but with this.'

He turned her and bent his head, his kiss warm, his breath against her mouth cool. Then his arms were roping round her, and his lips were demanding and strong, and even, yes, faintly cruel. Then they softened again, and he let her go, his expression unreadable. Abigail fervently hoped that, for once, he was unable to read hers, because it would tell him so much more than she wanted him to know.

Her emotions were in chaos, her thoughts in even greater turmoil. She had wanted that kiss, that embrace, that moment, to go on and on.

Passers-by smiled, averting their glances from the demonstration of love, as they would no doubt have interpreted it.

'That. . .' She had to clear her throat again. 'That was simply sealing a bargain, nothing else. There. . .' Now she needed to moisten her parched lips. 'There will be no love involved.'

'A business arrangement,' he agreed evenly, the roof of the bridge casting a shadow over his face as the sun moved down in the sky. 'No promise of love.'

He meant it, she was sure, but then so had she. Hadn't she? After all, he had a woman in his life, one who was far more sophisticated and accomplished than she, Abigail Hailey, would ever be.

And I just want a job, don't I? One that would enable her to stay much longer in Switzerland than she had ever thought possible on the day she had set out from her one-room apartment in London.

'We shall eat now, hmm? Come, Abigail.' He took her hand and this time she did not disengage it. 'We will look for a restaurant.'

He led her back over the bridge and, after a few minutes' walking, turned into a paved precinct, drawing her to a halt beside a café, outside which were scarlet-covered tables.

'This will suit?' he asked, still in possession of her hand. 'How big is your appetite?'

'Something light will be fine.' The hunger she had experienced earlier had been somewhat muted by the astonishing turn her life had just taken.

He helped her to a seat at a secluded table, then sat cornerwise to her, giving her a menu and taking another for himself.

Abigail studied hers in the light of the decorative lamps on the table. Around them, the shadows grew.

'Soups — they sound delicious.' Anything, she found herself thinking with a sudden upturn in her spirits, even a dry crust of bread, would taste like a mixture of honey and nectar at this particular moment. She did not seek to discover why; she simply let herself float on the tide of her feelings, enjoying every second, knowing that too soon it would all end. End in reality, she lectured her wayward thoughts, just as long as you realise. . .

'Yes.' She brought her thoughts to heel. 'My taste buds are already crying out for soup.'

'Spoken like a true Swiss, which you are not,' he commented with a smile. 'Soup-eating is deeply ingrained in the Swiss character. Packaged soups—did you know?—were a Swiss invention. Now here is one that I could recommend. It has everything—vegetables, pasta, meat, dumplings, cheese and potatoes. A meal in itself, in fact. A chef in any Swiss eating establishment will, as the mood takes him, experiment with savoury ingredients. Sometimes he will throw in almost anything—food, of course!—that his eye lights on.'

Abigail, her hunger growing as the minutes passed, could only smile and nod, her hands clasped in anticipation. Rolf summoned a waiter and ordered, then put his hand over hers, prising her left one away.

'No rings,' he commented. 'That must be remedied.'

She removed her hand, but he recaptured it.

'What did you mean,' she asked, frowning, 'when you said that the engagement was entirely private?'

'That only our immediate families should be told.'

'Such as Martina and Raymond?' He nodded. 'And your father?'

He straightened a fork that had been moved out of place. 'And yes, my father. It must be made plain to him in particular that the reason behind this arrangement is business, pure and simple.'

'Otherwise,' Abigail found herself challenging, 'he might tell the world? After all, you are his son and heir, as they used to say.'

A pause, then a dismissive lift of the broad shoulders.

Why, Abigail thought with a totally unexplained thrust of pain, isn't he honest enough to admit that he doesn't want his lady friend, Laura Marchant, to get to know?

'Which means,' Abigail declared, pulling at her hand, which he proceeded to hold even tighter, 'that a ring is most certainly not required.'

'On that subject——' he reached into his pocket, bringing out a small square box '—you and I differ completely.' With his thumb he flipped open the lid. 'This ring is not new. It isn't elaborate, nor is it conspicuous. It belonged to my mother.'

He removed it from the velvet-lined box. 'It's an antique piece, craftsman-made for my grandmother's husband-to-be. He gave it to her on their engagement. My grandmother gave it to my mother—she was the first-born daughter. It was offered to Martina, who didn't want it. The design offended her artistic judgement, she pronounced, and she gave it to me as the first-born son of the family.'

'Which means that it's a family heirloom,' Abigail commented, admiring the pearl and ruby and diamond setting. 'It should be given to—to the girl you do eventually marry.'

The silence was so long that Abigail glanced up. His blue eyes looked blankly back at her, eyebrows arched.

'Will you tell me something?' she ventured. 'Raymond told me about Beatrice, the girl you once. . .' The blue eyes narrowed, almost daring her to continue. 'You gave it to her?' He did not respond by so much as a flicker, but if he had felt for her as deeply as Raymond had implied she thought that he must have done. 'And in your eyes, as a result of her behaviour, that devalued it?'

There was the merest firming of the jaw, almost as if he was angry. 'I repeat, the ring was my mother's. Nothing could devalue it. Will you stop this prevarication? Not to mention the interrogation. Here.'

He eased the ring on to her engagement finger. It was an excellent fit.

'I shall take great care of it, Rolf. And I'll give it back to you the moment I book my flight home.'

He dismissed the matter with a brief nod, much as he would, Abigail reflected, the tying up of a business deal.

'You will want to inform your parents?' he asked, putting the box away.

She shook her head. 'My father died some years ago. And if I were to tell my mother she wouldn't believe it was a false engagement. Her hopes would rise, and I would hate to have to disappoint her.'

The wine Rolf had ordered was delivered to their table.

'Water for drinking,' Rolf informed Abigail while nodding his thanks to the waiter, 'hardly ever appears on a Swiss dining-table unless it is specifically asked for.'

Some wine was poured into their glasses and the remainder placed in an ice bucket beside the table. Rolf picked up his glass and inhaled the aroma, then took up the bottle and studied the label. 'A Riesling-Sylvaner. I hope you will like it.'

'I do,' she answered, wondering why the blood was singing in her veins and her heart leaping with happiness, but she had only to glance at the man sharing her table for her heart, pirouetting, to give her the answer.

The soup, with its sausage-meat dumplings, its variety of vegetables, pieces of egg and liberal helpings of pasta, was delicious. 'It's fantastic,' she told him, smiling into his eyes. 'You like it, too?'

He nodded, eyes hooded. 'Its flavour is enhanced, I must confess, by the company I'm keeping at the moment.'

'I know you don't mean it,' she responded with a smile. 'It's just a sentiment that goes with the situation.'

'Such as?'

'Well, false engagement, false compliment.'

He laughed out loud and the other customers turned, smiling indulgently.

They finished the meal with cheese and biscuits.

'Take your pick,' Rolf invited, indicating the chunks that were placed before them. 'This is *Gruyère*, and this is *Emmentaler*, the one with the large holes, or "eyes", as they are sometimes known. And this is *Sbrinz*, from the central area of this country. It is the hardest and oldest of Swiss cheeses. Which will you try?'

Abigail indicated the *Emmentaler*, at which Rolf,

taking up the cheese knife, cut a small piece and, wiping his fingers on the table napkin, popped it into her surprised mouth.

'Mmm, lovely nutty taste.'

'I'm glad,' he commented wryly, 'that you didn't seize the opportunity to have your revenge by biting my fingers.'

She laughed. 'Revenge for what? You surely don't mean the accident? I keep telling you. . .' She remembered that the last time she had tried to accept the blame his fingers had closed her lips. She remembered, too, how much she had liked their touch, wanted to move her mouth against them. . . His eyes as they rested on her were hooded, and she knew that he was remembering, too.

Afterwards, they wandered along, hand having spontaneously sought hand. They came across the giant chess set beneath the arches which Martina had pointed out.

'Can you play?' he asked.

'Not very well. As a child I remember my father teaching me and often letting me win.'

'Right.' He took her right hand in his, shaking it with mock-formality. 'A friendly match. I challenge you.' The look in his eyes as it flickered over the floral, figure-hugging dress she was wearing set her heart at trotting speed. 'A *very* friendly match.'

Abigail found it strange and amusing having to use her hands and arms to hoist the chess pieces into the required squares. Now and then he would come across and 'help' her, putting his arms around her, pretending to groan as if the chess-men were impossibly heavy. She laughed and shivered at the same time, liking the feel of his chest and hips against her back so much that it frightened her. In the shadow of the arches, he turned her head and took a kiss that made her heartbeat break into a run.

Rolf won, and the game was over too soon. They moved the large pieces back into their 'start' positions.

In the middle of the chess 'board' he pulled her into his arms.

'Thank you, Abigail.' His lips touched hers, then lifted, leaving hers unashamedly quivering for more. 'I've never—liked an opponent so much before.'

'Liked', he'd said, she pointed out to herself, just before he roped her to him and his next kiss blotted out not only their surroundings, but all rational thought. 'Liked'. . . Remember that, Abigail Hailey.

Her arms found their own way around his neck; her body moved of its own accord to make contact with his. Her breathing suspended itself as if to hold time still, so that the kiss would never end.

End it did, and for some moments Rolf stared into her face, picking out each and every feature as if to memorise them. Her hands clung wantonly to his shoulders, unwilling to leave the hardness of the muscle and strength they found there.

Fingers entwined, they wandered on. It was as if, Abigail mused, that 'engagement' they had arranged for their mutual benefit was real and enduring, leading the way to. . . She forced her mind away from the path it was taking. The engagement was a mockery; remember that, too, Abigail Hailey, she thought.

As they made their way back on foot to the hotel they passed the crowd which, though it was getting dark fast, continued to feed the seemingly ravenous birds. Some of them landed on people's shoulders; others pecked at scraps on outstretched hands.

Abigail hesitated involuntarily and Rolf, plainly feeling her faltering step, lifted one arm to rest around her waist, putting his other hand protectively on her head. Pulling her close to his side, they walked together, pushing through the group of people and emerging unscathed from the other side.

Smilingly, she thanked him. He smiled back, his arm firmly round her. No, no, she told herself, it's meaningless, this 'togetherness'; it's a dream. . .

Yes, a dream, Abigail was forced to acknowledge now, a dream which she wanted so desperately to become reality. She liked this man, she had to admit, more than liked him. Which was why, every time he kissed her — and it had this evening been alarmingly often — all her instincts drove her to respond to him, breathlessly and unreservedly.

The funicular was waiting and they stepped in, Abigail sinking to the bench seat, Rolf choosing to remain standing. There had been plenty of room beside her. He had not wanted to occupy it. End of dream, she thought; reality, here I come. If it hadn't been for the ring on her finger, she would have begun to believe that the two or three wonderful hours she had spent in Rolf's company had merely been the product of her imagination, too.

'Herr Felder, Herr Rolf Felder. . .' As they entered the hotel the receptionist caught Rolf's attention and he broke away, joining the woman behind the desk.

The conversation was in German, but when a tall, slender, blonde-haired figure emerged from the office at the rear, looking every bit as though she belonged, and placed a long-fingered, proprietorial hand on Rolf's arm, the language reverted to English.

'Rolf, you have deserted me,' the lady complained with a pout. 'Are you playing fast and loose behind my back? A *young* lady was with you, they said, when they last saw you, entering the funicular.'

If she hadn't already guessed the identity of the lady, Abigail reflected, her accent and her use of English would have told her. Without doubt, the lady was as British as she, Abigail, was. And her name, also without doubt, was Laura Marchant.

With polite deliberation, Rolf removed Laura's hand from his arm, and Abigail watched, taken aback, as he emerged from Reception and approached her.

'Thank you,' he said quietly, 'for a very pleasant evening. I will see you again soon.' With a nod and a slight, formal bow, he returned to his glamorous lady friend's side.

*   *   *

Disconsolately—she couldn't help it—Abigail walked towards the staircase.

'Hey, there, Abby.' Raymond's wide strides caught up with her. He placed himself so that she couldn't proceed. He stared at her, then his lips compressed. 'If that brother of mine has done anything to upset you. . .'

'No, no.' She summoned a smile from nowhere. 'Of course not. He showed me the town, gave me a meal. We walked.' After a long moment, 'We talked.'

'Talked? What about? You spoke as if it was something very important.'

Unthinkingly, she put up her hand to push her hair from her eyes, and he caught the flash of the ring.

'What's this?' He stared. '*That* ring?'

'What ring?' Martina emerged from the lift and joined them. 'Oh, that one. You must remember, Raymond. It was our mother's, and our father gave it to me. I didn't want it——'

'No sentiment about you, is there?' her brother jeered. 'For someone who prides herself on her artistic ability——'

'Don't equate lack of sentiment with lack of emotional response,' Martina reprimanded her brother. 'Rolf gave that ring to you, Abigail? Why?' She seemed sincerely puzzled.

'Abby,' Raymond exclaimed, 'you have not become *engaged* to the man, have you? You surely remember what I told you about him. . .'

He glanced around and pulled her towards the office to which Rolf had taken her. Martina followed, and the door was closed.

'He's got only one use for women, remember?' Raymond proceeded to remind her. 'He has this grudge against the female sex. He has never recovered from Beatrice's desertion of him for a much richer man. You can't have forgotten what I told you.'

I had forgotten, Abigail thought miserably, and now he probably thinks that of me, that all I want is position and money. How could she have fallen straight into his trap?

'You've got it wrong, both of you.' She had his permission to tell the family the truth. 'It's — it's not for public knowledge, but —— '

Martina brightened. 'A family mystery. Add interest to our mundane lives, Abigail,' she urged mischievously. 'Intrigue enters the Felder family. Tell us twins, Abby.' She put her hand on her brother's shoulder.

'The "engagement", it's not real.' Abigail proceeded to explain the situation.

'This work you talk about,' said Raymond, 'what has he conjured up to give you?'

She explained about that, too.

'So you are not going to be my sister-in-law,' Martina remarked, adding disgustedly, 'Which means that that woman Laura Marchant still has her claws in him.'

'But if he's got this grudge against women,' Abigail pointed out, 'how can she expect to make any headway? On a permanent basis, I mean. . .'

'She already has those two alleged requisites,' Martina replied.

Raymond nodded. 'Money and position.'

'Which puts her in the clear?' Abigail commented, her heart on its familiar downward trend.

'And in the running,' Raymond declared.

'Father's coming home tomorrow,' Martina informed her brother. 'Flying in from Vancouver. You will be able to meet him.' She smiled at Abigail. 'He's a peach.'

'What an expression,' her twin remarked. 'But, I agree, he's certainly a good guy.' His eyes grew sad. 'Never got over losing our mother.'

Martina nodded. 'Well, I'm off to bed. Goodnight, Abby.' Her expression became a little wistful. 'I wish that engagement was real. You would do fine as a sister.'

'Sister?' her brother exclaimed. 'My feelings where Abigail's concerned are anything but br —— '

'Please, Raymond.'

'OK, Abby.' A resigned shrug lifted his shoulders. 'But as I said, I'm good at waiting.'

'Look around, Raymond,' Abigail advised gently. 'There are plenty of other girls.' Like Liliane, Martina's new assistant, for instance, Abigail thought, but did not say, remembering the way Raymond had looked at her.

Abigail spent the morning wandering around the town. Posters on notice-boards attracted her attention. They pictured musicians from different parts of the world, many of them famous, who were coming to the town soon to take part in a music festival.

Turning out of a narrow street, she came upon the market. There were stalls filled with wholesome foods, fruits and vegetables. There were raspberries and black-currants on sale, she noted, along with corn, melons and cucumbers.

Pot plants and heathers stood beside dahlias and lilies, and jars held grasses waving in the gentle breeze. Petunias and roses vied with fuchsias and bulbs in bowls for pride of place on the wooden boards of the stalls.

It was a feast for the eyes, she thought, as well as for the sense of smell. She inhaled the aroma of the fresh produce, and heard the exclamations of pleasure of passers-by. Freshly made loaves of all shapes and sizes were proudly displayed inside glass or clear plastic covers, the yeasty scent tantalising the taste-buds.

Orange-coloured cloths covered a group of tables outside a nearby hotel, and Abigail took a seat. Coffee was all she wanted, and again her nostrils were teased with its smell as a cup was placed in front of her and the brown liquid poured into it.

As she drank, her eyes dwelt on distant spires and her ears registered the sound of ships' hooters from the lake a few streets away. She was, she acknowledged, storing up memories to think about when she was back on home ground. Feeling for the antique ring that Rolf had given — no, loaned — her, she could not help hoping that the moment of her departure could be put off, if not forever, then for some considerable time.

* * *

'Abigail, my father is home.' It was early afternoon now and Rolf stood at the foot of the stairs as she descended.

She had wondered what to do, knowing that Raymond was at work, and Martina was visiting stores in the town. She had not allowed herself even to hope that she would find Rolf somewhere. He, too, had his work to go to, besides fulfilling a busy role within the hotel's management.

Now he was here, in front of her, and her pulses leapt like new-born lambs. But new-born lambs grew up, didn't they, and stopped leaping? As she remembered the appearance yesterday in the hotel of Laura Marchant, and all that Raymond and Martina had pointed out about her position in life, those pulses abandoned their leaping and quietened down.

'My father would like to see you,' Rolf added.

'About the work?' He nodded and she followed him.

In the office, rising from behind a desk, was a tall, spare man, his carriage straight and proud, a characteristic which he had passed on to his elder if not his younger son. His keen eyes, again like Rolf's, rested on her as if making a lightning summing-up of her own character. Just like his elder son again, Abigail thought.

'Father, this is Abigail, Abigail Hailey. Abigail, my father, Anton Felder.'

Anton's hand extended across the desk. 'Miss Hailey, I am so happy to meet you.'

The pressure was less of a handshake than a gesture of paternal-like welcome, and it warmed her immoderately.

Arms folded, Rolf moved to stand near his father. His appraisal of her outfit — lightweight trousers and well-fitting embroidered cotton sweater — made Abigail feel uncomfortable, but she resolutely gave her attention to his father.

'Please be seated.' Anton gestured towards a chair. 'As my son may have told you, the chief interest of my life now that I have shifted the burden of management on to my son's shoulders——' a brief smile rested on

Rolf '—is the study of wines. And I have decided that it is time that I turned my attention to the wines produced in my own country. I hope to produce a book, and to do this I badly need the help of an intelligent young lady. Which my son assures me you are.'

Abigail's eyes flashed at the man in question, and his swift mocking glance in response brought the colour to Abigail's cheeks. His thoughts were plainly not simply of the business variety.

'You need someone to type, or rather——' Abigail indicated the computer '—print out your notes? In English, Rolf told me.'

'Exactly,' Anton Felder answered. 'You would be willing to do this work for me?' There was hope mixed with eagerness in his voice.

'Yes, I would, Herr Felder.' Her eagerness matched his and he seemed pleased by it. Her glance again bounced off Rolf. Dared she put the father in the picture without getting the son's permission? 'Did Rolf tell you. . .?' She extended her hand, revealing the ring.

'I did,' Rolf cut in, 'and he accepts and understands the position.'

'That the engagement is not real?' Anton commented. He smiled wryly. 'For once in my life, may I say that I would approve of Rolf's choice—if it were a true commitment?'

The statement in the form of a question was directed at his son, who had not changed his challenging and somewhat autocratic stance since the conversation began and whose expression now did not so much as flicker.

'Rolf,' his father went on, 'has made this stupid vow that, where emotional involvement is concerned, he will never trust a woman again.' He gave a faintly despondent shrug. 'One disappointment, and he allows that to rule his life. Heaven knows, he had the fine example of his mother and myself. . .' The catch in his voice stopped him. 'All the same,' he went on, 'it does make you one of the family, however temporary the arrangement may be. This is entirely acceptable to me.'

Abigail's eyes expressed her gratitude at Anton's generous and ungrudging statement.

He rose, coming round the desk and taking her hand. 'You cannot know how pleased I am to have your help. I shall be spending much of my time travelling the country, researching for my book, but already I can give you work. Here—' he led the way across to the desk on which the computer stood '—is a pile of notes. Would you like to look at them? Just to make sure,' he added with a smile, 'that you can understand my writing.'

Abigail complied, although Rolf had already shown them to her. Her smile met Anton's. 'Your handwriting is better than mine,' she commented, and Anton's head went back in laughter.

'Good. That is excellent. Now I must return to my suite and contact my friends and relatives in other parts of the country. I plan to stay with them, if they will have me, while I wander from town to town.'

Abigail glanced at the notes, then at her watch. 'Would it be OK if I started on these now? I mean, I was wondering what to do and. . .' She glanced at Anton, whose eyes lit up, then at his son, who nodded.

'I have an appointment in Zurich,' the son said.

'And I need to make those phone calls.' Anton gestured. 'On those shelves you will find all the paper you will need. Here, as you are aware, are the computer and printer. You see, Miss Hailey,' he said with a touch of mischief in his smile, 'it has all been waiting just for you.'

'Please, call me Abigail. After all. . .' With a daring glance at Rolf, she held out the hand that bore the ring he had given her.

'You mean you are my daughter-in-law-to-be?' He laughed out loud again. 'I like your young lady's impudence, Rolf. I am beginning to think that you may have taken on more than you realise in arranging this mock-engagement.'

Rolf's eyes narrowed. 'If her fantasy overrules her reason, then she must be prepared to take what comes.' He paused. 'In whatever form that takes,' he added coolly.

'Yes, well, your love-life — your *private* life,' Anton corrected, 'is entirely your own business.' At the door he added, 'I know you have already hurt this very pleasant young lady — yes, yes —' his hand stopped Abigail's instant protest ' — through no fault, maybe, of your own, but I just would not like her to get hurt in any — other — way.'

Rolf inclined his head and joined his father at the door. 'I believe there is no danger of that, Father. She understands the situation perfectly — for family knowledge only. Abigail?'

Abigail nodded. 'Your son already has a *private* life, Herr Felder. He doesn't need me. His. . .inclinations are, I'm sure, very well occupied elsewhere.'

'You see what I mean, Rolf?' Anton went out chuckling.

'You are provoking me, Miss Hailey?' Rolf said, a muscle jumping in his jaw. 'You wear my ring. In the circumstances, I suggest that it might be *prudent* of you to resist the urge to try my — shall we call it patience? — just that little bit too far.' He followed his father from the room.

CHAPTER FIVE

As THE afternoon passed, Abigail became deeply interested in the contents of Anton's notes. She had sighed with relief that he had at least numbered the pages, jumbled though they were. Sorting through them, she started to transfer them to the computer. They had begun,

My country, Switzerland, is noted for many things — for its watches, for instance, its machinery and its textiles and banking facilities, not to mention its mountains and ski slopes and the tourism they help it to enjoy. Not very much is known, however, of the regions where the vine is cultivated and where wine production has become an important local industry.

A telephone rang now and Abigail broke off to try and locate on which desk it stood. It was the one across the room which Anton Felder had occupied.

Heartbeats speeding — it had to be Rolf, hadn't it? — she announced, 'Abigail Hailey here. Hi, Martina.' Her heartbeats slowed. 'Yes, it's me. How did you guess?'

'I rang Reception. One of them saw you go into the office. Can you spare a few minutes? I've done the alterations to your dress. You remember the way to my workshop?'

'Hi,' she welcomed Abigail a few minutes later, 'try this on, will you? We-ell,' she exclaimed a few more moments on, 'isn't that just great? You like it, Liliane?'

Liliane echoed how 'great' it looked. Martina eased and smoothed the fabric over Abigail's shape, which the design of the dress emphasised, then awarded it top marks.

'If you'll remove it to let Liliane press it, you could wear it for dinner. Which is —' she looked at the wall

68

clock '—in about twenty minutes. You will dine with
Raymond and me, yes? Good. Now, while I tidy my
things, will you occupy yourself somehow?'

Abigail donned a robe from the back of the door and
wandered round, admiring the fabrics draped around
the place, their colours, their bold patterns and the
smooth feel of them.

'You're very clever,' Abigail remarked on a sigh.

Martina laughed. 'I could turn coy and deny it.
But——' head high and with a broad smile '—being a
Felder through and through, I'm inclined to agree. But
I have trained to degree standard in the subject. And
I've travelled—to your country, too—learning techniques. You——' she was closing opened boxes and
gathering scattered sewing accesories '—have probably
got a hidden talent—a creative one, I mean. Most
people have. That's my opinion, anyway. Your hands,
they're long-fingered. Do you ever play the piano?'

Abigail was pulling on the dress which Liliane had
ironed. She paused, surprised. 'You're very discerning.
Yes, I can play. I had lessons as a child and teenager. I
passed music exams, but I'm no concert pianist.'

Martina nodded, going to help Abigail with the zip
fastener. 'There isn't room for everyone at the top.
There,' she said, looking with some satisfaction at
Abigail's reflection, 'it's perfect for you. You have a
good figure, Abby. I know of one person who has
noticed.'

'You mean Raymond, of course.'

'Do I? Raymond, yes, he misses little about ladies'
shapes. But no, I was thinking of. . .never mind. He
won't be there this evening.'

Abigail's heart did a dance, but it soon ended. She
could not have meant her elder brother. But Martina
was right, she thought, looking in the mirror; it did a
lot for her, that dress. It was turquoise and purple,
combining with soft greens. The predominant colour,
however, was blue, matching her eyes. Its neckline was
wide, its cut revealing curving attractions which the
loose-fitting clothes she usually wore tended to hide.

'Mmm,' commented Raymond as he escorted them into the restaurant. 'Who is this attractive stranger, Martina? I'm sure I have seen her before, but. . .' He laughed, trying to capture Abigail's hand. Ostentatiously, she lifted that hand. It bore Rolf's ring, and Raymond groaned. 'OK, signal received, but when that symbol of betrothal, false as it is, is returned to its owner. . .'

They had just reached their table and were studying the menu when Abigail felt her eyes drawn to the entrance.

The new arrivals paused, and the man's eyes, blue and unreadable, clashed with Abigail's. His companion, tall and slender, stood with a half-smile, surveying the scene.

Who else would Rolf's companion be but Laura Marchant? Abigail asked herself, frightened by the thrust of jealousy that speared through her.

'Our usual table, Rolf?' Laura asked, her English tones carrying across the restaurant. Without waiting for an answer, and as if she knew every inch of the way, Rolf's guest swayed towards the window and stood by a chair.

Rolf helped her into it, then took the chair across from her. That way, Abigail deduced acidly, he could gaze into his lady friend's face, studying every feature, noting her every mood change and adapting his own accordingly.

'Her Highness makes sure,' Martina commented sarcastically, after giving her order to the waiter, 'that every eye is turned to her. But her taste in clothes — yuk. OK——' she studied Rolf's companion with professional eyes '—so she probably spent a small fortune on that outfit. But it *kills* her colouring. The fashion assistant must have been thinking only of her commission when she convinced Laura, as she obviously did, that it suited her. Why,' she addressed her brother, 'does Rolf's taste in women friends have to be so *abysmal*, Raymond?'

'Why ask me?' was the brotherly reply. 'Pure guesswork, but I imagine it's because he's just playing with all those female "friends" of his, with no intention of making a commitment. You've known his views ever since Beatrice left him for her millionaire.'

'Look how hard she's trying, though,' remarked Martina with a grin. 'She doesn't know she's hammering on a locked—not to say bolted and padlocked—door. The one to his heart, I mean.'

Abigail was angry with her own heart for taking such a dive at Martina's words. On no account, she tried to tell it, must it lose itself to the man across the restaurant, the man who, for convenience's sake, had slipped a ring on to her engagement finger.

Towards the end of the meal, Raymond took her hand, and, because Rolf was at that moment smiling at something his lady friend had said, Abigail allowed Raymond to keep it.

'*My* heart isn't locked, Abby,' Raymond said, head on one side. 'You can have it any time, you know that.' He lifted her hand and put it to his lips. His sister snorted at the exaggerated gesture. 'You,' he rounded on her, 'have no feelings, no romance inside you. All you like is work. You and Rolf, you are a pair.'

'Talking of work. . .' Martina said, pushing away her coffee-cup and rising from her chair.

Raymond gave Abigail back her hand. 'You're going to your work-room?' he asked his sister. 'Will Liliane still be there? Then I will go with you.'

Abigail had to suppress a smile at Raymond's sudden transference of interest from her to another girl.

'Abigail? *Abigail*.' They were passing Rolf's table but, head high, Abigail ignored his peremptory summons.

Why should I run at his call, she asked herself, when I'm sure that all he wants to do is introduce me to the real object of his desire, making quite sure that I understand just how meaningless and temporary our 'engagement' really is?

* * *

A few minutes later, the view from her window, misting and golden as the sun started to descend, called her irresistibly. She became conscious of a restlessness inside her, a need to get away.

In the lift she realised that she had forgotten to take a jacket, but decided that, as she would not be going far, it was not worth her while going back for one.

'Abigail.' It was a command she could not this time ignore, simply because the man who had uttered her name so abruptly was standing in her way. Without pushing him—and anyway, he was stronger than she was—she knew she would not make it past him to the exit, so she headed round him for the door to the office.

He was there first, opening it and pulling her in before she could change course and escape. She broke away and made for her desk, pretending to look through his father's notes.

He turned her and she propped herself against the desk's edge, then wished she hadn't, because his eyes skated over her, dwelling on the shape which Martina's clever design had revealed, on the swell below the neckline, on the way her hair skimmed her shoulders.

'More beautiful,' he murmured, trailing his fingers over the white skin of her throat, 'without the dress, beautiful though it is.'

So he had not forgotten seeing her when she had shed the dress for Martina to adjust.

'Why,' he asked, his mood altering, 'did you pretend to be deaf to my request in the dining-room?'

She could bluster, she thought, allege that she had not heard him, but he would guess she wasn't speaking the truth.

'You only wanted to introduce me to your lady friend,' she parried. 'You assumed too much—that I actually *wanted* to meet her. I expect she knows about us. After all, it's only natural that you'd want to tell your very close friend the truth about us——'

'She does not know about us,' he grated. 'She is not family.'

Yet, Abigail wanted to say, but did not dare.

A step brought him even closer, until he was pressing against her so much that she had to put up her hands and hold on to his shoulders for support. She gritted her teeth and kept to herself the pain of the bruises the impact of his car had inflicted. She should have known, she told herself, that he would notice her reaction, but he had reached the wrong conclusion.

'What's wrong?' he clipped. 'You prefer my brother's touch, especially when he kisses your hand? You do not like the feel of my body against yours?'

She bit her lip. 'It's not that, it's. . .'

He lifted himself from her and at once she missed the pressure of him, the excitement of his nearness that had already begun to make her skin tingle. 'Those bruises I saw on your body when you were changing in Martina's work-room, they still trouble you?'

'Sometimes.'

His manner softened just a little, his arms going round her, gathering her unresistingly into them. To her dismay, she could not find within herself an atom of protest, nor the slightest wish to evade the kiss that was now a mere breath away from her lips.

They let her down, those lips, parting almost as if they were eager for his take-over, allowing him to touch them open even more. The intrusion that followed was so heady, so arousing, that it awakened her body to clamouring life. All this — it can't be happening, she thought. It *must not* be happening, because there was no future in it, only today, now, with no tomorrow to come. No promise of love, he'd said. Remember that, warned her saner self.

He had lifted his head and was staring into her eyes.

'Tell me now,' he growled, 'that you like my brother's kisses more. I know that you and he have been closer than you want the world to believe. I know that you lived in the same house for a year ——'

She broke free, tugging back her hair. 'But not the same bed,' she cried. 'You know nothing. Raymond doesn't have *your* morals, nor do I. He waits until he's invited. . .' She could have bitten her tongue.

'So you admit he means more to you than the friend you are always proclaiming that he is.'

'I don't, I don't.' She raced to the door and dragged it open, slowing down for appearance's sake as she crossed to the exit.

He caught her up. 'Where are you going?'

'For a walk. Please don't follow me.'

He did not follow; he walked beside her to the door.

The funicular was standing empty. She would, she decided, shut the sliding door on him and press the button before he could join her, but his name was called from the reception desk. She heard a smothered curse and glanced over her shoulder to see him disappear into the office at the rear.

Slowly pacing the promenade, she turned and gazed up at the Hotel Panorama Grand. It stood high on the cliff. No wonder, she thought, its funicular from ground-level was so well used. And no wonder the guests in those rooms had such a fine view of the lake and mountains. Its red-tiled roof and attractive chalet-style architecture fitted in perfectly with the high, tree-covered hills beyond and above it, and with the other similarly styled buildings around it. No modern high-rise buildings here, Abigail thought thankfully.

By counting the windows, she could just pick out her own room in the hotel; its scarlet blind, partially pulled out over the balcony where, most mornings, she took her breakfast, afforded protection from the sun's rays. It matched those over every other window, an attractive splash of colour on every one of the numerous floors of the building.

Turning back towards the lake, she hugged herself, the tremble that had taken hold after Rolf's kiss had ended still persisting. She *must not* let him get to her; she *must* remember what Raymond had told her about Rolf's cynical and twisted attitude to women. His kisses, devastating though they were, meant nothing, *nothing* — the end-product, she told herself cynically, of years of practice on his part.

Finding a bench seat in the shade of a tree, Abigail

stared unseeingly at the rippling waters. The massive beauty of the surrounding mountains was gilded by the evening sun. Boats lifted and fell minutely on the tiny waves, their sails furled, masts pointing emptily towards the pale blue sky.

Something drew her eyes to the left, and her heart jumped when she saw a man standing at the water's edge, hands in pockets, staring down, a man whose physique filled her with longing, whose arrogant manner both annoyed and drew, whose kisses transported her to a place very like paradise. . .until they ended and she crashed down to earth, whimpering.

He had not seen her, she was sure. He would surely expect her to have walked some distance by now. She rose to take that walk, but her name hung on the air and she was no longer alone.

As he walked beside her, she noted through her side-vision that before leaving the hotel he had shed his business suit. He now wore jeans and an open-necked shirt over which he had pulled a blouson jacket.

She considered breaking away, but knew his long legs would soon catch up with her, so she continued to walk, head high, pretending that he was not there. Nor did he break the silence, until they reached the centre of the town. Moving to the kerbside, he put his arm firmly around her waist, tightening it when she showed signs of resisting.

'Let us cross here. It is dangerous, is it not——' his lips quirked as he glanced down at her '—for a man and a woman to indulge in a stand-up fight in the middle of a busy road? Besides, remember what happened the last time you plunged unthinkingly into fast-moving traffic.'

She stifled her protests and allowed him to guide her across to safety. When she tried to detach herself from his hold, he turned her. His face was tantalisingly in shadow.

'Will Abigail Hailey pretend for a while,' he said softly, 'that Rolf Felder is friend, not foe?' She could not suppress a smile. 'That is better, *Liebling.*'

'Darling', he had called her. But it had rolled off his tongue, hadn't it? she calmed her racing pulses, as if the word had been used many times to many different women.

'Now we will walk. You don't object to climbing, and not only hills? Good, so this is the way to the city wall.' He took her hand, turning away from the lake and making for another part of the town.

In no time they were approaching fields, where cows were scattered, pulling at the grass. The cowbells clanged and rang, making heavy but strangely tuneful sounds, telling of peace and tranquillity and a slower pace of life.

They reached the base of the great wall where it spanned the roadway, its arches lifting the ancient stone structure over the modern traffic.

'The steps over there ——' Rolf indicated a long flight upwards ' — lead to the base of one of the towers. Are you game to try?'

'Why not?' She rose to his challenge. 'I may look fragile, but I'm tough,' she added with a smile. 'After all ——' with an impudent sideways glance ' — I stood up reasonably well to being knocked down by you — er — your car, didn't I?'

His hooded eyes carried out a quick all-over survey of her figure. 'I would need to — shall we say, do another check on the state of your bruises? — before I could go along with that statement.'

She knew what he meant, and her body's response to his words shook her composure deeply.

'The answer is no.' She softened the negative with another smile.

'Yeah? You think? I think differently, Miss Hailey. Before many hours have passed, hmm?' His calculating expression and the masculine anticipation it contained made her shiver inside, not with fear, but with an excitement that both stimulated and frightened her.

If this man really put his mind to seducing her, from where would she dredge the strength to resist him? Dismayingly, as each moment had passed, she had enjoyed more and more being in his company. Every time she looked at him something happened to her sensual responses, and more worrying still, to her emotions. . .

Following him as they climbed, Abigail did her very best to keep up with his confident strides.

'The wall was built around 1400 and there are nine towers in all,' Rolf told her as they paused for breath after climbing one staircase after another, some circular, some made of wood, 'and each of its towers is different. See,' he added, breathing deeply, they reached the top, 'this tower is square, with a pointed, red-tiled roof. Another has a turreted wall with miniature 'spires' on each corner. Yet another along the way has its own kind of spire with twin spires emerging out of that.'

'Are we really at the top?' she queried, panting. 'I thought we would never get here.'

They started walking along the wall, and Abigail gasped at the view that met their eyes. To one side was the old Chapel bridge, where the river it spanned fed into the lake. The lake itself reflected the gold of the sunset, the summits of the mountains, range upon range of them, lit with scarlet and gold.

As they turned to go back, Abigail felt Rolf's arm go round her waist.

'No, don't move away,' he said huskily. 'I am friend, not foe, remember.'

She looked up at him, head on one side, seeing gilt sun-flecks in his blue eyes, a half-smile curving his sensual lips, and the sweep of his strong jaw.

He pulled her to his side. 'Down there, I have to admit, I wondered if you would make it to the top.'

She looked up at him. 'You really thought I'd plead for mercy and say, Let's turn back?' Dared she add it? 'What sort of women have you had as lady friends, Herr Felder? Beautiful in face and figure, but limp and weak when it came to physical activity?'

A sharp pat on her rear brought indignant colour to her cheeks.

'Provoke me at your peril,' was his growling rejoinder as he gazed down into her rebellious face. 'Remember that this is mine.' He lifted her hand which bore the ring.

'It doesn't make *me* yours, too,' she retorted. 'That ring has no real significance.'

'Any time I am willing — more than willing — to give it "significance". Just say the word, *Liebling*, and I will oblige. Your room or mine, the choice is yours.'

Her cheeks, deeply red not only from the sunset colours, came into the possession of his cupped hands. As his mouth descended she heard him murmur, 'It would not be difficult becoming your lover.' Then his mouth, ungentle now, took hers in a kiss that from the start was intrusive and seeking and ruthlessly demanding.

His free hand pushed through the opening of her dress, possessing a breast, the pressure rough, the flick on the nipple slightly cruel. A shuddering gasp escaped her, her breathing ragged and jerky, but he took it into him, showing no mercy.

When he finally let her go, all resistance had drained from her and she lay in his arms, staring up at him. He looked into her eyes and she longed to read his thoughts, but it was in man-language, with no interpreter around to come to her rescue.

He eased her upright then, holding her beside him, turning her to gaze on the gilded waters of the lake far below, the orange-coloured sky, the nearer hills, dark before the night took them altogether, as it had already taken the distant mountains.

'Isn't it beautiful?' Abigail whispered, a catch in her throat.

'Beautiful,' he agreed but, as she glanced up, she saw that his eyes were on her.

As they ascended to the hotel entrance in the funicular after walking back through the town, Rolf's hand having captured hers, Abigail, seated, watched unseeingly as the lower floors of the building went by. She caught a glimpse on a lower level of Martina, busy in her work-room, but no sign of Raymond.

Rolf again had not joined her on the seat. Instead, he had stood, hands in pockets, feet planted firmly for balance. Abigail felt he was looking at her, but did not trust herself to look back at him, for fear of giving her feelings away. It was those feelings, strengthening by the minute, that gave her the greatest cause for concern.

Don't, something in her cried, don't whatever you do fall for the man. He's beyond your reach, never mind the fact that the ring he gave you — no, *loaned* you — is on your finger. Nor must you fool yourself that his kisses on the city wall meant any more than a passing satisfaction of his masculine appetite, and even, perhaps, a demonstration of his ability to conquer any woman, even one who was determined not to succumb to his charms.

Was determined? she questioned herself. Wasn't that just a bit too late? Hadn't she already allowed herself to do just that? Be honest, her reason lectured her emotions, and admit that you've fallen for the man, fallen so hard that no other man will ever, in the future, fill the place Rolf Felder already occupies in your heart.

Raymond greeted them as they had pushed through the swing-doors into the hotel. He stared first at his brother, then at Abigail. Rolf's arm did not at first drop away. It was almost a gesture of challenge, a kind of statement. . .you've lost out, Brother. OK, so she's just another woman to me, but what of it? I have her; she's mine.

In a strangled voice Raymond declared, '*Sie ist meine Freundin!*'

'*Oh, ja?*' Rolf responded with a tight smile. Then, so that Abigail would not mistake his meaning, 'That's what you think.'

His name was called and his arm dropped away. He sketched a small bow in Abigail's direction — its formality chilled her to the heart—and entered the office behind the reception desk.

'What did you say to Rolf?' Abigail asked Raymond.

A heavy shrug, then, 'I told him that you were *my* girlfriend. Come, drink with me, Abby. I've spent a lonely evening.'

'I thought you went to Martina's work-room to see Liliane?' Abigail asked with mock-innocence.

'She'd gone home.'

So, Abigail thought, keeping her smile to herself, he wanted me as a substitute and I was not around. She followed him into the bar and he bought drinks, knowing her taste from his friendship with her in England.

He toasted her a little lugubriously. 'To Abigail, to her common sense, and long may it keep her from my lecherous brother's clutches. Abby,' he said more seriously, 'stay away from him. I told you the score. He'll have love-affairs by the dozen, but he'll never make a commitment, not to any woman. Now I. . .' His smile was hopeful and coaxing, but Abigail shook her head. She knew better, that his eyes, and his emotions, were not for her alone.

All the same, she could not trample on his feelings, so she covered his hand with hers. He turned his palm and took her hand in his. He was so nice, she thought, so very pleasant, yet he was not for her. But the man she knew now that she really wanted—whom, she had to admit, she *loved*—was not for her, either. So where did that leave her?

CHAPTER SIX

SLEEP evaded Abigail for so long that she stopped trying and, having taken a shower, she stood at the window, but failed to find the tranquillity she sought by gazing at the view over which the sun had completely set now.

Lights were strung like beads along roads that climbed; neon signs advertised names of Swiss-made watches so famous internationally for their quality and precision that they really needed no promotion.

Her mind was in a turmoil, her body too stirred and restless to let her rest. Rolf's kisses were still with her, her mouth still throbbing, her lips even now wanting more of them.

The discovery that she had fallen in love with Rolf Felder, and so deeply that it reached into her inner being, had shattered her peace of mind. The awful truth that faced her from now on was that the parting of their ways was quite inevitable and that, as a consequence, her mind's peace would never be restored.

'Abigail.'

The sound of his voice stung like an electric shock. Wrapping her towelling robe more effectively about her, she answered croakily, 'Yes?'

'Will you let me in?'

How can you let him in, a voice inside her cried, when he only has to lift a finger and you'd go running — right into his arms?

'Abigail!'

She caught her breath. His voice was authoritative, demanding. She would not respond, do its implied bidding. Except that he was not just any man, he was part of the hotel's management, and she was aware that if she did not do as he wished he would repeat his demand, regardless of whether or not he was overheard

81

by other guests. So she opened the door sufficiently to whisper, 'Will you *please* go away?' She had not switched on the lights, and her eyes lifted to a face in shadow.

His answer was to shoulder the door's opening sufficiently wide to allow him entry, then he leaned back against it.

He looked her over, seeming to like what he saw, the shape of her body outlined against the faint light coming from the world beyond the window.

'Why did you try to keep me out?'

Suppose she told him, I now know that your body is so irresistible to mine that I can't trust my reflexes, let alone my emotions, to keep you away from me any more than that door succeeded in doing?

He lifted himself upright. 'Maybe you would prefer Raymond in my place,' he grated. 'I glanced into the bar this evening and saw the way he held your hand and that you had not only not tried to stop him, but had covered his hand with yours.'

It was only because I didn't want to hurt his feelings, she could have told him, but knew he would have laughed in disbelief.

'I suspect,' he went on, 'that you and he became more than just the "friends" you claim you were while you lived in the same house.'

'You're wrong,' she asserted, her hands agitatedly seeking the robe's belt and tying it. As she had loosened her hold the neckline had fallen open a little, revealing a curve of pale breast. A curse in Swiss German escaped him.

'So what,' he exclaimed, 'if I am second-best in your eyes?' He seized her by the forearms, swinging her round so that the floodlighting which shone on to the building played over her face. 'You will discover that I am more *adult* in my intimate approach, more experienced in my *romantic* ways.'

His kiss was ruthless and mind-shattering, swamping her thoughts, overcoming her resistance.

When she felt his hand push open the neckline of the

robe even more, she sought desperately to restore that resistance, but could only cling to him helplessly.

When his palms began to push at the collar of her robe and find their way inside to slide over her shoulders, then move to discover the satin smoothness of her breasts, she could only gasp at his audacity, then shiver at what the touch of him on her heated flesh was doing to her.

Stop him, stop him now, her reason pleaded; he only wants you for his own selfish reasons. It's no use, she argued silently, I simply don't want to stop him. So she turned her back on her rational self, giving in instead to the intense feelings that were welling up inside her under the soft, insistent caress of his hands, the plundering of his lips and tongue as they teased and circled her now uncovered breasts.

Head back, she closed her eyes, feeling the eager responses of her body, loving his arousal of her desires, moving her as no other man had ever done before.

'Abby, Abby,' he said huskily, 'do you know how beautiful you are? Has no one told you what you do to a man?'

It was like the rumbling of distant thunder on a bright summer's day, a warning, reality breaking through, reminding her. . . No promise of love, he had vowed, when he had suggested the false engagement that would enable her without difficulty to tackle his father's work.

'Abby, stay away from him', Raymond had urged. 'He'll have love affairs by the dozen, but he'll never make a commitment, not to any woman'.

She struggled free of his hold, uncaring that his eyes seemed to be transfixed by the piquant shape of her breasts, her hands trembling as she pulled the robe back into place.

'So what if I'm "beautiful"?' she challenged, crying inside, because her greatest wish was to let this man make complete and total love to her, and because she knew that if she did she would be unable to hide the truth from him. 'I mean no more to you than any other woman you've had in your life. Raymond warned me.'

'Ah, yes.' His eyes narrowed and his hands slid into the waistband of his jeans. 'I forgot about Raymond. One day, you — or he — will tell me the truth about your relationship. And I mean the truth.'

A protest had sprung to her lips, but he was already at the door.

'Tomorrow,' he said, turning, 'I shall be in Zurich. The day after, I'll be free. I intend going up into the mountains, partly on business, partly for relaxation. Since you have so far seen little of this area, would you like to come with me?'

The invitation had been so coolly given, his manner so remote, that she needed almost to pinch herself to make sure that it was the same man who had, only a few moments ago, taken her in his arms and kissed her so passionately.

All the same, her heart lifted more than a little at the thought of spending a whole day with him, fraught with emotional danger though it might be.

'Thank you,' she answered with a coolness which, she hoped, matched his. 'I accept your invitation.'

'Good.' His tone was brisk and businesslike. 'Be ready after breakfast, will you?' He named a time. 'Goodnight.'

Before she could answer, he was gone.

The next day seemed endless. She spent most of it working on Anton Felder's notes, and as she worked she became immersed in them.

She picked up the telephone and ordered morning coffee, then returned to her desk. The notes informed her,

It should be remembered that the way of life in Switzerland is like that of other Continental countries, in that wine is generally served at the two main meals of the day. Where an Englishman would drink beer, or an American would choose 'Coke and rum', the Swiss prefer two 'decis' of white wine.

When the tray of coffee was carried in, she nodded, making a space on the desk and continuing with her work. The notes continued,

The sale of the year's wines is held in November. Buyers and hotel owners come from far and wide to buy the produce.

As she worked, the fact that the newcomer had not knocked, requesting permission to enter, registered on her mind. She looked up questioningly and Martina burst out laughing.

'I wondered how long it would take you to surface,' she remarked. 'I did not want to disturb your concentration.'

With something like relief, Abigail swung away from her work and poured the coffee into the two cups provided.

'I intercepted the tray,' Martina explained. 'I was coming to see you, anyway. Thanks. No sugar. I am aiming to get my figure down to your measurements.' She made a face at her own shape. 'Some hope, unless I stop eating altogether. Talking of measurements——' she swung a chair round so that she faced Abigail '—that's why I have come. This afternoon, could you spare some time from my father's work to do me a favour?'

'Well, yes,' Abigail answered cautiously, 'if I'm able to.'

'Oh, you are, and it's nothing too difficult. Just lend me yourself to try on some of my models. The girl who usually does it has suddenly taken herself off for a holiday.'

'Leaving you high and dry?'

'Right. She's promised to be back in time for the party we're giving when the house is ready for occupation. I told you about that, didn't I?'

Abigail nodded. 'You're sure I'm the right shape? I mean, her shape?'

'I know your measurements from that dress of mine Rolf bought for you. I sent him the bill, did I tell you?'

she added with a grin. 'He said — his words — "As long as I get my money's worth, I don't mind". Now what, I wonder, did he mean by that?' Head on one side, Martina smiled mischievously.

Abigail cursed the colour that flared, trying to suppress the memories of his kisses the night before. 'I just don't know,' she answered to the sound of Martina's renewed laughter.

Lunch over, Abigail made her way down to Martina's work-room. The trying-on session lasted some while, but she did not mind, because the clothes she wore, if only for fifteen minutes at a time while Martina adjusted them, were so attractive that they made her feel good and forget her tiredness.

Raymond burst in, work over for the day. Abigail did not miss the fact that his first glance was for Liliane, who coloured a little at his entrance. There were two or three other employees working there, at the numerous sewing machines, or cutting out shapes from the fabrics that Martina had designed.

'Hi, friend,' Raymond saluted Abigail. 'I see that my sister hasn't taken long to talk you into helping her, too. The Felder family is really making use of you, isn't it? My father, with his notes on wine. My sister.' He gestured. 'My brother.'

He did not seem to notice the sudden warmth in Abigail's cheeks.

'Pretending,' he enlarged, 'that you're engaged to him to put Laura Marchant in her place.' He couldn't possibly guess, Abigail thought, how her heart had sunk at his words. 'I guess she's been getting too demanding lately, probably making pointed remarks about settling down with none other than Rolf Felder, the only man she knows who could provide her with the worldly goods to which she's accustomed, not to mention an endless supply of money her bank account would love to have poured into it.'

'He's sworn never to marry,' Martina reminded him.

Raymond dismissed the statement with a shake of the head. 'Laura's no fool; she'll find a way one day.

She's got everything going for her; even you can't deny that, Martina.'

'Yuk,' said Martina. She moved away, surveying her handiwork. 'That's fine, Abby. Thanks a lot for your help. If I need it again. . .?'

'Just as long as it doesn't interfere too much with my work for your father.'

'That's great. Raymond, on behalf of the Felders, thanks a lot for bringing your friend Abigail over here to stay for a while.'

Raymond bowed elaborately. 'Any time,' he said. He whispered, under cover of the noise of the sewing machines, all three of which were now being used, 'Just as long as she doesn't take seriously her engagement to my brother Rolf.'

Abigail could not do justice to the delicious breakfast that had been delivered to her room. She had toyed with the food, her appetite having been overtaken by the excitement that filled her at the thought of spending the day with Rolf.

The mere sight of him leaning languidly against the reception desk, on the guests' side for a change, sent her heart into a spin. He wore cotton trousers and a navy casual shirt, a jacket suspended by its hanger from one forefinger. His hair was wind-blown, as if he had already taken a walk. He looked alert and vital, supremely fit and, she reflected, hurrying a little, if not exactly impatient, then raring to go.

Their eyes met as she descended the stairs — the lift had been too long in coming for her to have the patience that day to wait — and there was a kind of detonation inside her, like a coming together of chemicals that were so combustible when combined that a shattering explosion resulted.

It's true, she thought, as she advanced towards him; it's a question of chemistry. And magnetism. Look how he's pulling me towards him. I couldn't resist him even if I tried. And she had to admit that she wasn't trying one little bit.

She dropped her key into the appropriate opening in the countertop. Rolf took her hand, leading her towards the funicular. Just before the entrance door swung to behind them, his name was called. He heard it, halted, swore faintly, then walked on.

'My day off,' he stated firmly, 'is my day off. Free of duties, free of responsibilities.'

'You told me,' she reminded him, 'that you were combining relaxation with work.'

'What are you——' arms folded, he smiled down at her as they descended to street-level '—besides pretending to be my betrothed—the voice of my conscience?'

Waiting to cross the busy street, Rolf put his arm protectively around her. 'We'll walk into the town, yes? Then I can make the excuse to hold you tightly as we pass the place where people feed the gulls and swans and assorted bird life. Hmm?'

She laughed up at him and his arm resumed its place around her waist.

The lake had never looked so intriguing, so mysterious as it did now in the morning mist that hid the mountains and clothed the lake-craft in gossamer-like veils. Rolf booked them on to a ferry and, as they waited for the boat to cast off, he looked at her, smiling faintly.

'There is a glow about you. Does the thought of going to the summit please you so much?'

She could not tell him the actual truth, so she nodded.

Standing at the boat's rail, she told herself that it was a day she would remember for years to come. So what if the heavy mist persisted? Rolf was with her, and he provided all the brightness she needed to light up the day.

Beneath her feet was the throb of the engines. The lake's surface was calm and the gulls flying around the boat were looking for titbits and wanting more and more, appetites never satisfied. Like mine for Rolf's company, she thought dreamily, watching him standing a few paces away as he stared at the slowly emerging shape of the mountains.

Other ferry boats went busily by, criss-crossing each other's wash. A strong breeze picked up, playfully lifting Abigail's hair. Rolf joined her, stroking the tendrils back and putting his arm around her waist, and she thought the day could hardly offer a greater happiness.

The boat travelled fast, and Abigail commented on it.

'It's diesel-powered,' Rolf told her. 'It's not strictly a pleasure boat, although it carries tourists, of course.'

'Your country is beautiful,' she sighed.

Rolf smiled. 'I may be prejudiced in its favour,' he commented, 'but I do have to agree with you. You know it's divided into cantons? Twenty-three of them, in fact, and three of those are subdivided into two half-cantons. That is, they're small sovereign states with their own laws and parliaments.'

'And yet you're *one* country?'

'You're surprised at what is called our "unity in diversity"? It goes back many centuries to when the peasants of different cantons felt the need to safeguard their traditional rights against the claims of foreign powers, and so they vowed to stand by one another.'

'In these parts,' Abigail observed, 'the chief language seems to be German.'

'A form of German, yes. The spoken language in this region is *Schwytzerdütsch*, but with German, or *Hochdeutsch*, as the written language. But no less than four national languages are spoken in the country as a whole. Plus many local dialects, of course.'

The ferry boat made for a mooring jetty and houses, which made up the small settlement they were rapidly approaching. Abigail watched as passengers left and others came on board, then the boat moved away, continuing its journey.

Low wooded hills gave way to rougher terrain, and Abigail stood in silence beside Rolf as the boat made for yet another jetty. It slowed and moored, secured by ropes.

'This is where we disembark,' Rolf said, taking Abigail by the hand and leading her towards that deck's exit.

The journey upwards was by cog-wheel train, which Abigail found fascinating.

'Did you know,' Rolf remarked, 'that the Snowdon Mountain Railway in Wales, which was built towards the end of the 1800s, was designed by a Swiss engineer?'

'No, I didn't.' Her eyes invited, Tell me more.

'On both axles of the locomotive of those trains there are cog-wheels — or pinions — which engage with the track. It was pioneered here in Switzerland. The loco-motives were ordered from Switzerland, also.'

As the train climbed, it stopped at garden gates and schoolchildren with their cases and bags jumped on, running out along garden paths from their homes and their waving parents. At other stops people thrust out their hands and, as the train slowed down, new passen-gers jumped on. With the gradient as steep as it was, the train did not once come to a complete halt.

'You need to be agile in these parts,' Abigail com-mented with a smile, 'to get on and off these trains.'

Rolf laughed and agreed as he sat beside her. 'We are proud of the fact that this is the oldest cog-wheel train in Europe.'

'This,' she gestured, 'is fantastic. The slope is so steep.'

'A one-in-four gradient,' Rolf told her. 'In other words, a steepness of twenty-five per cent. Incidentally, you might be surprised to hear that the engineer who built this had to fight to get financial support. Can you see the contraption on wheels at the front? Inside it are supplies being taken up to the hotels and the people who live here.'

The train halted at a passing-place, then moved on. A voice gave instructions to the driver — by radio, Rolf explained. At the top, they found the sun again, and blue sky and a brightness that dazzled.

'We've climbed above the clouds,' Abigail exclaimed,

pointing to the far-away mountaintops that pushed through the white and grey blanket.

Rolf nodded. 'On a clear day you can see mountains into the far distance — the Mönch, for instance, the Jungfrau and the Eiger, which are reached from Interlaken, about a two-hour train ride from here. Now,' he said as they left the train and walked even higher towards the terrace of an expensive-looking hotel which perched near the edge of the panoramic view, 'I will see you to a seat where you can enjoy the sight of this —— ' his arm swung widely ' — while I go inside and, I hope, do business with the management. We are hoping before long to take this particular hotel into the Felder group. You will be OK?'

Abigail assured him that she would and, when he had disappeared into the building, opened the menu and studied the items offered. After a while a waiter approached, asking for her order, switching to halting English.

'My — my friend.' She gestured. 'I'll wait for him, thanks.'

'Herr Felder — your friend? Ah,' he said nodding as if he comprehended, 'he will be back soon.'

Abigail gazed around, admiring the view all over again, misty though it was. Children played, their voices and shouts to each other echoing, floating, escaping the confines of the hotel complex to the mountaintops beyond. Flags flew, rippled by the breeze, all different in design, no doubt representing, Abigail surmised, the different cantons of which Rolf had told her.

There was a stillness all around which the chatter and the childish cries only seemed to accentuate. It was, she mused, as if the mountains out there were only tolerating the sounds of humans until dusk and dark descended, when their own massive silence could then be reimposed.

Rolf returned, striding to the table, seizing the menu and reading it aloud. He had not told her the result of his discussions, but then, she reflected, feeling for the mock-engagement ring, it was really none of her business.

'Let me see,' said Rolf, '*St Gallen Bratwürst mit sauerkraut und Kartoffelsalat* — grilled St Gallen sausage with potato salad. Yes? Or *Gebackene seefisch fillets salzkartoffeln?* That, translated, is fried lake-fish fillets and boiled potatoes.'

'Yes, please, I'd like that.'

Rolf summoned the waiter and gave their order, at which the man nodded deferentially as he went away.

'He's very polite,' Abigail observed with an impish smile. 'Was your business meeting successful? No, sorry, forget I asked.'

He moved the table-ware around. 'The matter under discussion came to a very satisfactory conclusion. OK?'

'Good. And thanks for not telling me it was none of my business.'

The meal was served, accompanied by the grape juice that Rolf had ordered for Abigail. Hunks of delicious bread came with the main course, and as Abigail sank her teeth into her portion of bread Rolf laughed and complimented her on her strong jaws.

Four young men, quilted jackets discarded, booted feet at rest while their gear lay around them, sat talking or dropping off to sleep.

'Have you, like them — ' Abigail nodded in the young men's direction ' — climbed in these parts?'

'Yes, I've climbed in these mountains. And others further south.'

'When I was in the town the other day,' she commented, watching his profile, sharply etched as it was against the mist-bound, snow-capped peaks, 'I saw some posters advertising a concert.'

He nodded. 'Did you know that we, as a nation, love music? You, also? That, at least, is something we have in common.'

'Laura — Laura Marchant — does she like music, too?'

When his cold eyes turned her way, she wished she could have slid under the table. But she couldn't have stopped herself if she had tried. What I really wanted him to tell me, she acknowledged silently, was that Laura meant so little to him that he did not know her likes and dislikes in such matters. When *will* I stop hoping for the impossible? The 'impossible' being, of course, a reciprocation of her love for him, a love that seemed, distressingly, to be deepening with every passing day.

'Sorry. I've said the wrong thing again. It's not my business.'

'Don't apologise. I hear the influence of my brother and sister behind that question.'

'Are you going?'

'To the concert? I am. You, too, are going. I have bought a ticket for you.'

She longed to ask, Is it the one you bought for Laura, but she couldn't go with you? Instead, she thanked him. 'I'll pay for that, of course, when I——'

'When you inherit a fortune from a non-existent rich uncle?' he teased, taking her hand. 'It is paid for, Abby.'

Back in the hotel, Rolf followed her into her room.

'You're comfortable in here? I should have arranged for you to have a suite. I shall ask them to move you, yes?'

'No!' she exclaimed, aghast at how much a suite would cost. 'Thank you,' she remembered to add, 'but I won't be staying here long enough, will I, to make it worth while?'

'You won't? You are intending to break your promise to my father and walk out on his work?'

Shocked, she answered, 'Of course not. That isn't what I meant.'

'What did you mean?' He smiled into her eyes and her heart did a secret dance. There was a warmth in his eyes that threatened to melt her defences.

'I meant——' she began, but his arms came around her and to her dismay she found herself going into them as if her body was convinced that it belonged there, feeling his breath on her throat as his lips touched hers, lifted, then touched again. Tiny impulses shot up and down her spine and she shivered as his mouth found her ears, her cheeks, then finally her mouth.

Her lips seemed to have been waiting for his for so long that they quivered even as he used his own lips to part them. As he started to familiarise himself all over again with the taste of her, and she of him, she forgot the fact that he had another woman in his life, one who was far more suited to his position in the world, but who was willing to accept a relationship with him on his own terms—with no commitment and *no promise of love*.

She forgot everything, except that he was there again, in her life, assuaging her longing for him. Until then, she told herself, she had not realised how very deep her feelings for him had gone—so deep, in fact, that she knew for certain she would never be able to uproot him from her thoughts, even when he had irrevocably gone out of her life.

He lifted his head and, with his fingers around her chin, tilted her head upwards so that their eyes locked with each other's.

'Before long,' he said thickly, 'I will come to you. I warn you, *Liebling*, you will not be able to keep me out. I want you, Abby, you cannot guess how much.'

Shocked, she pulled away, indicating her hand. 'It means nothing, this ring, which also means that there's no real connection between us. You have no right——'

His eyes had hardened, his lips becoming a thin line.

'You allow me to get this far, lady——' he was coldly angry now '—before you start putting up the barriers? And "no right"? Where do *rights* come into it, into the relationship between a man and a woman these days? And "no connection between us",' he quoted her bitingly, 'when there's this *electricity* whenever we touch, this pull? For me, it overrides everything else, every other consideration.'

He spoke the truth, she could not deny it, but how could she tell him it was exactly that 'pull' that made her so afraid? She found it—him—so irresistible that she could hardly bring herself not to fling her arms around his neck every time he ended a kiss and beg for another, and another. . .

'No promise of love', he'd said, she reminded herself fiercely. And it was love, warm, emotional love—alongside the physical love which was all he was offering—that she wanted most of all. It was by a sheer effort of will that she kept her expression blank and unresponsive.

He swung on his heel and went to the door.

'Rolf.' He half turned. 'Thank you for a very enjoyable day.'

She gazed into his eyes and willed him to relent, but his jaw firmed and he left without a word.

CHAPTER SEVEN

'WOULD you like to come with Raymond and me up into the mountains?' Martina asked Abigail. 'You have worked so hard for the last two days, shut away all alone in my father's office, that we think you badly need some fresh air.'

'Anyway, it's Saturday,' Raymond pointed out, appearing behind his sister at Abigail's door. 'Even working men like me——' he attempted to pat his own back '——need a break.'

'The mountains are not exactly of the white-peaked variety,' Martina went on, dropping into one of Abigail's chairs. 'Not at this time of the year, anyway.'

'Just lead the way and I'll follow,' Abigail told them with a smile. It was a relief in itself to find her lips curving upwards instead of maintaining the straight line that her low spirits had dictated since Rolf had left her two evenings ago.

'Rolf,' said Martina, as if reading her thoughts, 'is busy with his own business concerns. You know he has this engineering firm in Zurich? Well, his lady friend has whispered some warnings in his ear, it seems, and he's taken them seriously. Warnings about his company, I mean. Not warning him off. That's the last thing she'd do. The thought of his bank account is too attractive to her for her to want to ditch him for lack of commitment.'

They joined the train at the station. The carriages sat as calmly, Abigail thought, as if for their entire journey they would be moving over flat land. But this, Raymond had assured her, was certainly not the case.

At first they rode along the lakeside, passing among chalets and houses which, her companions told her, were mostly divided into apartments. There came a high-pitched train whistle just before they entered a

96

tunnel, emerging into a different kind of scenery with fields which, among the largely hilly ground, managed to maintain their level surfaces.

The train rose out of the valley and soon they were among the mountains, the hill slopes forested and green. Some chalets perched precariously on steep inclines. Cows grazed, the sound of their bells varied and musical.

'Sets of cog-wheels have taken over,' Raymond explained, 'from the ordinary wheels. It's called Riggenbach's cog-wheel system, which is how the train is able to cope with the very steep gradients.'

They arrived at last, strolling past shop windows and along cobbled streets where, overhead, balconies protruded, filled with flowers. The Swiss national flag was proudly displayed, draped over the street and hardly moving in the still air.

'I'll see you two later,' Martina announced, hoisting her portfolio into a more comfortable position under her arm. 'I have this customer to see. She lives in one of those apartments up there, and she's wanting to choose one of my fabric designs for an outfit we are going to make for her.' With a wave, she disappeared into the building.

Abigail looked around her. Encircling the town, its altitude already high, were majestic mountain peaks, row upon row of them, their shapes carved by erosion and the passing of time. Their presence dominated the town, drawing the eye up to their summits, to marvel and admire.

'In the winter,' Raymond explained, 'this place is a ski resort, so don't be fooled by the greenness. They're not tame, those mountains, and you have to be skilled in the sport before you can even begin to tackle the climb.'

Many of the shops, Abigail noticed, displayed ski and sports wear geared to icy conditions.

'We're a thousand metres above sea-level here; that is, for your benefit,' he added with a smile, 'roughly three thousand, two hundred feet. It's a summer resort, too. Also the starting-point for mountaineering expeditions.' He indicated some young men wearing jackets and boots and warm clothes, with bulging packs on their backs.

'They're aiming for those mountains?' Abigail asked doubtfully.

Raymond nodded. 'At this time of the year,' he replied, 'they're tame to people like that. You should see those slopes in winter.'

Abigail nodded, imagining.

Martina rejoined them and they went to Raymond's favourite restaurant for lunch. He had a long chat with the waitress, whom he knew by name, while Martina made notes and Abigail absorbed the atmosphere of the place and the sight outside of shop windows and tourists passing and, above them all, the great mountains rising in beauty and in challenge.

For a while afterwards they walked in a park, taking a seat for a while to listen to the band which had made itself comfortable on the bandstand. Abigail's eyes strayed upwards, this time to the green hills which formed the backdrop to the park. Chalets, wide-roofed and balconied, climbed one on the other up the slopes, which at the top were fringed with a thick line of trees.

The sun had disappeared and it had begun to rain as they started their descent in the train.

'The series of concerts begins in a few days,' Martina remarked, placing her portfolio on the seat beside her, while Raymond occupied the place next to Abigail. 'You will be coming with us, Abby, won't you?'

Abigail nodded. 'Rolf has bought me a ticket.'

'The concert, the first one,' commented Martina's brother, 'she can't forget it. Do you know why, Abby?' The smile which he directed at his sister was intended to taunt. 'The man she fancies is one of the performers.'

'Raymond!'

For the first time, Abigail saw a discomfited Martina, one who blushed and displayed embarrassment.

'She's trying to deny it,' Raymond persisted, 'but his name is Otto Kaufmann. He is an up-and-coming pianist. You've probably seen his picture on the posters in the town.'

'Dark-haired, dreamy-looking?'

'That's the one. "Dream" is right. He's Martina's dream, isn't he?' he prodded his silent, pink-faced sister.

'What if he is? I've only ever seen him from a distance. But,' Martina admitted with her old smile, 'I have to admit I would dearly love to — to shake his hand.'

Her brother laughed. 'You never know your luck. We might find that one of the concert organisers is willing to take you backstage and introduce you to him when the music's over.'

Martina became lost in thought, then, 'If you haven't got anything special to wear for it, Abby——'

'I simply can't accept another one of your creations, Martina — at least, not without paying for it myself. And I really couldn't afford your prices, much as I would love to.'

'OK,' Martina answered matter-of-factly. 'Just as long as you realise it's a special occasion. There's a world-famous orchestra——' she named it '—in addition to the pianist. You know, the one I fancy. That should please you, Abby.'

Raymond, puzzled, asked why, so Abigail told him. 'Nothing to do with the pianist. It's just that I told Martina I play the piano. Well, let's say I used to. I had lessons, but when my father died the money ran out.'

At dinner, Abigail shared a table with Martina and her brother. They moved into the lounge and talked until Martina yawned and Abigail had to force herself to stay awake. Raymond saw Abigail to her door.

'I guess,' he remarked ruefully, 'that the way into your life is as barred to me as your——'

She put a finger to her mouth. 'Don't, Raymond. Don't spoil our——'

'Beautiful friendship. OK.' Her door was half open now. 'But a kiss isn't forbidden, is it? Between friends, I mean.'

He proceeded to kiss her in a way that made her
want to push him from her. With immense restraint,
again not wishing to hurt his feelings, she tolerated it
and even managed a smile when it was over.

'There,' he said in an amusingly soothing voice, 'that
didn't hurt, did it?'

Yes, she wanted to say, but shook her head instead.
She did not know just how much it had 'hurt' her until
Raymond went on his way and she entered her room,
closing the door behind her.

A gasp escaped her and a shiver took hold. A man half
lay, half sat in her chair, his legs extended, his arms
hanging loosely over the sides. He seemed totally
relaxed, if not actually asleep. . .until she met the ice
in his slitted eyes, saw the obstinate jaw thrust forward.

When he spoke, however, he made no reference to
what surely could not have escaped him. Or perhaps it
had, Abigail reflected, hoping against hope that this
guess was right.

'I'm sorry to have given you such a shock,' he
remarked, 'but I'm tired to my bones. And when a
man's in that state he kind of gravitates to wherever —
or whomever — he believes will understand and sym-
pathise. Or did I get it wrong?'

His eyes closed and his head hung back, and he did
not seem to want an answer.

'How did you get in?' she asked.

Eyes still closed, he felt for and held up the master-
key. 'I did the forbidden thing and let myself uninvited
into a guest's room.' The key was pushed back into his
pocket, and one eye opened. 'Are you going to complain to the management?' The eye closed again.

She smiled and looked at him, loving the length, the
strong build of him, the wide shoulders. . .the hard and
handsome face, the well-shaped lips, the thick brows
that emphasised the deep blue of his eyes.

On an impulse that she would have controlled had
she herself not been so tired, she crossed to his side
and, putting her hand behind his head, gave it support.

The mere touch of his hair on her palm, the weight of his head in her hold, made her skin tingle, her responses spring to life.

In a moment he was on his feet, pulling her to him and stifling her cry of alarm with his mouth, parting it and invading and taking its moist sweetness into his keeping.

'So you're open for business, Miss Hailey?' he rasped. 'First with the younger brother, then, having told him goodnight, sent him packing, probably pleading tiredness, but in reality being more than ready for the older brother.'

She struggled from him and swung her arm, but her aim was diverted by the swift reaction of his hand grasping hers before it made contact.

'You're insulting me,' she cried. 'You're loathsome and I hate ——'

His lips were hard and ruthless, pressing against hers until she was forced to allow him access, then intruding once again on her inner lips, the secret cavities, testing, probing the yielding softness, until her legs threatened to sag under his mouth's erotic demands and she was forced to cling to him to prevent herself from sinking to the floor at his feet.

When his head lifted at last, her lips throbbed and she was breathing as if she had run up the side of a mountain. Her gaze locked with his, her body pulsating with a driving need that made her close her eyes and fight against it before it revealed to him her deepest feelings, her very love for him.

'Abby,' came from him huskily, 'don't fight me. Not tonight. If I'm angry with you, it's because ——'

'I know why!' was wrested from her. Because of Beatrice, he had been going to say. 'Raymond told me. But will you believe me when I tell you that yes, I've spent the evening ——' his eyes began to harden again '—the *evening*, not the *night*—with Raymond. And with Martina. We talked for hours. That's all.'

'So I imagined that kiss outside this door?'

She had to be honest; she had to shake her head. 'I

didn't want him to, but, well. . .' She frowned up at
him; how would he take her words? 'He's sweet and
gentle, and I didn't want to hurt him, so. . .'

His displeasure showed, which meant she had failed
to convince him, but he seemed to sag and sank down
into the chair again, this time pulling her with him. She
sank with total relief into the strength of his arms.

He tipped her chin and rubbed the ball of his thumb
over the fatigue-induced shadows beneath her eyes. 'I
can be sweet and gentle, too, Abby.' She looked up at
him, laughter in her eyes. 'You don't believe me? I'm
not a cardboard cut-out, *Liebling*. I'm flesh and blood
and I'm tired to my core. I've been involved in a fight —
no,' he added with a smile, 'nothing physical, a financial
fight. Someone I know alerted me to the danger.'

Abigail thought, And I know who that 'someone'
was.

'There's been a take-over bid for the Felder group of
hotels,' he confided. 'Thanks to my — friend —' oh,
how that hesitation hurt, Abigail thought ' — I was told
in sufficient time for me to take action to prevent it,
and the Felder company is safe. I flew to the south of
the country, then drove for miles to see my father and
confer with him. I flew back two hours later.' He closed
his eyes. 'I had a long and bitter two days. Abby,' he
whispered, 'refresh me, restore me to life.'

His arms around her tightened and hers found their
way around him, too, and a sigh came from the depths
of her. Her forehead rubbed against his cheek, feeling
the prickly shadow, but not minding it. At that moment
she wanted nothing more in life than to stay there being
held by him.

Smiling, she glanced up and found that his mouth
was moving towards hers, and she accepted without
question just what it signified. She wanted to feel the
hard line of his lips on hers, catch the musky scent of
him, feel his arms like bands of steel close round her
compliant body. . .exactly as it was happening now.

The kiss seemed to have no end, deepened, in fact,
making her press closer. She put up no resistance at all

when invading hands cupped her burgeoning breasts. She did not lecture her body when it yielded to their slow, demanding caress, the stroke of his breath on their sensitised flesh as his tongue circled their throbbing peaks. A gasp was drawn from the depths of her when his fingers pushed down through the waistband of her jeans and started a slow, tingling exploration of the uncharted territory beyond.

A small voice told her that she shouldn't be lying there in a state of near-surrender to a man who had cut commitment to any woman from his list of life's ambitions. Ignoring the warning, she burrowed even more deeply into his heated embrace, feeling his aroused response and disregarding the small signals of warning that tried to make themselves heard.

His arms were male and muscled, and she had no desire at all to tear herself away from them. He lifted her face, and she saw the light in his eyes and wondered how much longer she would possess the strength to deny him the intimacy he would soon demand.

He rubbed his fingers over her cheeks and put his mouth on hers. Her lips parted involuntarily and he found the now familiar path to her mouth's inner sweetness, his tongue seeking and finding the tiny pulses that beat inside her upper lip.

'Your own special scent, *Geliebte*, my treasure; it drives me nearly insane. I want to feel you. . .' He opened his shirt wide, then unfastened her blouse, peeling it from her shoulders. 'I want to feel your smooth skin, your beautiful shape, against me. You understand how a man feels when the woman he desires — has been desiring for all the long hours of his absence — is there at last in his arms?'

Her bra followed her blouse to the floor and she turned to him, her breasts making intimate contact with his chest, which felt hard against them. Her breaths came faster as she felt the zip on her jeans give beneath his tugging fingers, his hand invading and stroking and, finally, resting against the quivering skin of her stomach.

'I shall stay here——'

'Please, no.' It was a cry from the heart, meaning, I know you want me, and I want you, but if we went all the way I would never forget you, and I *have to* forget you if the rest of my life is going to be worth living.

His teeth snapped and she thought he would tip her off his lap and walk off, taking his anger with him. He did no such thing. Instead, a sigh, part annoyed, part long-suffering, escaped him.

'A man,' he said at length, 'can take so much, but beyond that. . .'

She yawned into his neck and he laughed, turning it into a growl as she rubbed her face against his cheek.

'OK, OK, so I'll wait. But not for long. And——' his gaze became threatening '—if you dare to tell me again that I have no rights, by letting me even get as far as this——'

'I didn't mean to provoke you,' she whispered.

'No?' was his unbelieving response. He shifted a little to accommodate her slowly relaxing body, and she fitted herself more comfortably into the muscles and angularity of him.

She awoke to a feeling of being carried. She was being lowered to the bed and a cover was drawn over her. She became aware that she was wearing very little now, and she held out her arms for Rolf to join her.

She was only dimly aware that he was kissing her, certain that it was a dream. When she heard the door close, she sensed that she was alone, but was still convinced that she was dreaming. How could Rolf have gone, after the wonderful things he had said to her?

There was a voice in the corridor—Rolf's voice—responding to the two-way radio which Abigail had noticed he sometimes carried around with him. He had clearly been called away urgently. But he had kissed her lingeringly before he left. She had that, at least, to hug to her when she awoke, alone, in the morning.

Martina rang her room next day. 'Have you bought yourself an outfit yet?'

'For the concert? No,' Abigail answered, 'but I've got a dress I brought with me. . .' The caller had gone, having cut herself off.

Four minutes later there was a tap on the door. Martina swept in so fast Abigail had to step back.

'No arguments, Abby. This is an outfit from my collection. I am not sure about it, and I would like you to try it out in public for me. Please.' Her smile was almost as disarming as her elder brother's. 'I shall trail you all evening with my notebook and pencil, making notes of people's reactions to it. You will do this favour for me?' She did not wait for an answer. 'Come, try it on.'

Abigail laughed, giving up, giving in.

'A perfect fit,' Martina sighed. 'Like the proverbial glove. Have a look at yourself — no, at the outfit, I mean.'

The top was of gold Lurex jersey and faithfully followed her shape. The scarlet long-sleeved jacket, its edges decorated in the gilt glitter of the top, matched the fitted skirt that curved around her hips and tapered to her calves.

'Here,' said Martina, diving into a bag, 'these will finish off the outfit.' She drew out a necklace that consisted of row upon row of large red, amber and black beads, and a similar long bracelet intended to be twisted many times around the wrist. 'Good.' Head on one side, she asked, 'You won't back out now?'

'OK,' Abigail replied with a sigh, 'for your sake I won't.' She studied her reflection. 'It's just great. It does things for me. Even these —' the beads at neck and wrist ' — are a perfect foil.'

'That's settled, then. And afterwards it will be returned to the rack of clothes which I have especially designed for the house party. It's coming along well, the house. Did you know? Soon we — the family — will be moving in.'

Which, Abigail thought, leaves me out in the cold.

Martina frowned. 'Do I read you right? Are you already mentally packing your bags to go home? You

will still be needed in the Felder household, will you
not, to do my father's work?'

'But——'

Martina tutted crossly. 'Abby, you cannot go away.
You are the only barrier there is to that hateful Laura
Marchant's really getting her claws into Rolf and
making him marry her.'

It was Abigail's turn to frown. 'I can't see it that
way.'

'While you're wearing that ring,' Martina pointed
out, 'he can't make any public commitment to Laura.
Don't you see?'

Abigail's heart lifted a notch, then she reminded
herself firmly that privately he could. It was only a
family secret, after all.

'Thanks,' she said, 'for the loan of this outfit.' Then
with a touch of mischief, 'I'll take care not to spill
anything over it.'

Martina pretended to growl, clenching her fists. 'If
you do I'll. . .' She waved herself from the room.

CHAPTER EIGHT

THE pile of notes had grown, Anton having sent them by post and by fax machine. Abigail worked for the next two evenings, telling herself that, that way, she wouldn't miss Rolf so much. He had disappeared from view again, Martina having told her he had returned to Zurich and, also, that he wasn't alone there.

'That *woman* Laura Marchant is with him, would you believe?' Martina had added.

So the wonderful episode in his arms had meant absolutely nothing to him, Abigail thought, so little, in fact, that he had put her out of his mind and taken Laura into it, and into his bed, too, probably, she reflected despondently.

On the evening of the concert Raymond called into the office and told her that he and Martina would wait for her downstairs in the reception area.

'Rolf hasn't returned yet from Zurich,' he informed her, 'but it doesn't matter, because Martina and I will look after you.'

Descending the stairs slowly — the lift had been too busy for her to wait for it — she sought in vain for her two friends. She frowned. Maybe she was early, but she had judged the time of her arrival almost to the second.

She was on the bottom step when a man emerged from the shadows. The world seemed to spin. She stumbled and he was there, steadying her with his hand on her elbow.

He had never looked so cool, so heartbreakingly masculine, nor so handsome. His dark evening clothes, the bow-tie, the whiteness of his shirt, all combined to underline the finely fashioned features.

'Where — where are Raymond and Martina?' she asked, hoping to hide her pleasure at seeing him by distracting his attention.

107

'They have gone on alone.' His eyes became hooded. 'You would rather be escorted to the concert by them?'

'No,' she replied too quickly, so she attempted to sound casual. 'No, of course not. It's just that ——'

'You were expecting them to be here. They told me. I said I would do the honours.'

His eyes raked her slender figure, and a soundless whistle came through his teeth. 'There is only one occasion,' he commented with a half-smile, 'when you have looked more beautiful than you do tonight.' Eyebrows arched as she flushed. 'You can guess? Yes, I see that you have.'

She wished he could not read her face so easily, and, through that, her thoughts and feelings.

'Your sister,' she told him as he led her towards the funicular, 'she persuaded me to wear this. It's from a collection she's going to show at the party when the house — your family's house — is finished.'

The funicular was waiting. They stepped in and the door closed. 'I guessed this ——' the movement of his hand indicated the outfit '— might be the work of Martina.'

'She said she wasn't sure of it and asked me to do her a favour by wearing it.'

Rolf laughed. 'I have to hand it to her; she's clever, and not only artistically. She fooled you. Once it has been worn, it will no longer be new. Nor would she allow one garment of her own design to appear in public unless she *was* "sure of it". Her aim was to show off her handiwork in the context of a social gathering which might well include a number of ladies with rich husbands, to whom she could say, Yes, it's beautiful, isn't it? It's one of mine. And yes, I'm open for business!'

Abigail laughed. 'I really don't mind. In fact, I'm honoured to be wearing a Martina design.'

'Did it not occur to you,' he queried softly, 'that it might be Martina who was being honoured — by your consenting to wear one of her models?'

They had left the funicular and were on their way to the underground car park.

'Definitely not. I'm just an ordinary working girl, except that, back home, I wouldn't be working. I'd be without a job at present. Who is Abigail Hailey, when compared with the rich customers Martina caters for?'

He showed her into the passenger seat and manoeuvred the car out of its parking place and into the evening sunshine.

'You have no ambitions in life beyond finding a job when you get back to your own country?'

Two things lowered Abigail's spirits from the high level of excitement they had reached. First, that he seemed to be completely reconciled to her leaving at some time in the near future; and second, the possibility that he might be testing her attitude towards the 'position and money' he had once pronounced were, without exception, the sole aim of the female of the species.

They drew up outside the concert hall and Rolf handed the keys to a waiting attendant. The car was driven away for parking.

Abigail could not help being just a little overawed by the building, with its line of stone arches stretching right and left. Baskets overflowing with flowers were suspended from each archway, adding colour and a delicate perfume which hung on the quiet evening air.

Rolf's arm around her shoulders ushered her into the entrance foyer of the concert hall. Tickets were passed on the nod, raised arms were waved in his direction, while others in the crowd pressed his hand. One thing was certain, Abigail thought — Rolf Felder was not only well known among the people of the town, but popular, too.

She was aware of being appraised with some curiosity; Rolf introduced her merely as a friend of the family, which, she told her foolishly disappointed self, was only to be expected, wasn't it?

The atmosphere, to the uninitiated, and especially to a foreign visitor as she was, was just a little overwhelming. A glimpse into the auditorium revealed gilt-painted, scarlet-seated chairs, dark red carpets with a luxurious tread, and, sparkling over it all, a series of brilliant chandeliers.

Women guests had risen to the occasion, wearing dresses and jewels that told of large bank accounts and of wealthy husbands' generosity. This was, it seemed, one of the most important events of the year, and the townspeople had dressed accordingly.

How right Martina had been, Abigail reflected, glancing down at herself, to 'exhibit' her work on such an occasion, and in such a highly charged atmosphere, even if it was only she, Abigail Hailey, who was acting the model.

The words 'Festival of Music' were printed in large letters on long banners set high around the walls.

The pressure of Rolf's hand on her shoulder and a murmured apology as an acquaintance literally dragged him from her left Abigail with the feeling of being lost in a crowd—until a shout attracted her attention and a raised arm indicated the presence close by of Martina and Raymond.

She pushed her way through to them, and it was Raymond's arm now that rested across her shoulders.

'My bad-mannered brother deserts you,' he declared; 'so I, Raymond Felder, will retrieve the family honour and escort you in his place.'

'It wasn't Rolf's fault,' Abigail began. 'Someone grabbed his arm and——'

'Don't try and defend him. Anyway, *I* am your friend, your *true* friend, not my brother. Forget that ring, Abby. I keep telling you, it means nothing.'

'Worse luck,' bemoaned Martina. She wandered away, Abigail following, with Raymond trailing after them. Martina paused in front of one of the tables which were set to one side displaying compact discs and recorded cassettes. On some of them were photographs which Abigail recognised as being of one of the evening's soloists.

'Look at my sister,' Raymond commented in a stage

whisper, 'ogling the picture of Otto Kaufmann, the solo pianist, the man of her dreams. See, she's buying one of his cassettes.'

'Will you be quiet,' Martina exclaimed without heat, staring with something like longing at the picture on the label. 'One day,' she sighed, 'I'll just have to meet him.' A bell rang. 'Come on, you two, we must make our way to our seats.'

Abigail cast one hopeful glance over her shoulder in an effort to catch Rolf's eye, but she was impelled away by an impatient Raymond.

'Forget him,' Raymond directed. 'He's obviously forgotten you. He's probably talking business. I told you before you came here that he was a workaholic. He and my sister are two of a kind. You see——' as Martina turned to Abigail and realigned the chunky beads around the neckline of the glittering top, then rearranged the drape of the jacket just a little more tidily '——here she is, working even now. This is one of yours, isn't it?' he asked his sister. 'I thought so. Now these are our seats, and here, Martina, are our numbers. Rolf's seems to be the gangway seat.'

There was so much to see and to admire in the great assembly hall. Gilded balconies, layer upon layer, massed with flowers, rose towards an ornately decorated ceiling. Velvet drapes were looped away from the front of the curved balcony seats in which people were talking and laughing and settling down.

Raymond had supplied them each with programmes, and Martina became absorbed in its contents, the page bearing Otto Kaufmann's photograph being left open, and at which she gazed. Abigail studied the programme in a desultory way, her mind being more on the empty seat beside her. She found herself becoming more and more restless at Rolf's failure to appear.

Even when the members of the orchestra filed in to take their places in the great semicircular area below the platform there was no sign of him.

'Why don't you put that cassette away?' Raymond

taunted his sister. 'Can't you bear to have it out of your sight?'

'No,' was Martina's measured response, craning her neck to try to discover if Otto was there in the midst of the orchestra.

'He's the soloist,' Abigail leaned across Raymond to point out, 'which means he won't appear yet.'

It was as the lights were being lowered that Rolf finally appeared, taking his seat beside Abigail. She fought but lost the battle to keep her heart out of her eyes.

'Unavoidably detained,' Rolf said quietly. 'A cliché, but true. I'm sorry to have left you alone like that. You have missed me?'

'Not really,' she lied with a secret smile, at which he passed a fist playfully near her chin.

'I escorted her to her seat,' Raymond put in. 'After all,' he continued with a concentrated frown, 'she is *my* girlfriend.'

'Raymond, I ——'

'OK,' he conceded, 'it's neither the time nor the place for a heart-to-heart. Nor for a quarrel with my brother.'

A great quiet descended on the auditorium, and the conductor of the orchestra lifted his arms. Angled beams shone on the players, flooding them with a bright white light. The music took over and Abigail forgot everything, except that Rolf was beside her.

Towards the end of the first half the conductor left the rostrum, reappearing with the soloist. Applause broke out at the mere sight of the bright-eyed young man, who bowed from the waist.

'Oh, heavens,' Abigail heard Martina breathe, 'I can't take my eyes off him. He's so grand, so— fantastic.'

Martina, Abigail thought with astonishment, always so collected and down-to-earth, was in the process of losing her heart to someone quite beyond her reach. During the performance, Abigail wondered if Martina had remembered to breathe.

When the applause broke out, Martina's hands out-
clapped them all. 'His playing,' Abigail heard Martina
comment to her brother, 'it's out of this world.'

It was the interval, and Rolf led them through the
surging crowd to the bar, pushing through and buying
them drinks. Raymond looked around, while Martina
became engaged in conversation with a young woman
in the crowd.

Rolf made to talk to Abigail, but at that precise
moment someone attracted his attention, and Abigail
knew that once again she had lost him.

'Yes,' Martina was saying, 'I'm the fashion designer
Martina, of Martina Models.' They shook hands. 'Quite
by chance, I have a friend from England — here she
is —' she beckoned to Abigail '— who is wearing one
of my designs. You don't mind, Abby?' Martina whispered in her ear.

Abigail shook her head. 'I agreed to do you a favour,
remember?'

'It's just great,' the young woman declared. 'I sure
like the colour combination and the — well, the whole
impact.' She felt in her evening bag. 'I have a pen
here. . .' It seemed to elude her.

'Please,' said Martina, 'I'll give you my card.'

'Hey presto,' Raymond murmured in the background. 'Quite by chance, of course, she is carrying her
business card. Martina's nose is to the ground, as ever,
scenting new custom.'

'The interval bell has sounded,' Rolf informed them,
reappearing. 'We must return to our seats.'

Martina had changed places with Raymond and now
sat next to Abigail. It was during Otto Kaufmann's
performance of Beethoven's Fifth Piano Concerto that
Abigail discovered that Martina was crying. Whether it
was with sadness that she would never meet the man of
her dreams, or the beauty of the music that had moved
her so deeply, Abigail told herself she would never
know.

As it ended and the rapturous applause broke out,
Martina, having mopped her tears, jumped to her feet

and clapped madly along with the rest of the audience. Abigail was relieved to see that her friend had returned to her normal well-balanced self.

At Rolf's suggestion, and through his contact with people who had connections with the concert organisers, they joined the milling crowd behind the scenes. Abigail noticed that Martina had taken her newly purchased cassette from her bag and was clutching it to her, her eyes searching eagerly for the main soloist of the evening. Was she hoping, perhaps, to obtain his autograph?

The young woman who during the interval had shown such an interest in Martina's designs approached them and introduced herself now as Sylvia Hafner, an American married to a Swiss businessman.

'Please,' she said now, gesturing, 'let me introduce you to my brother.'

Abigail swore she could feel the leap of Martina's heart. Then Martina swayed and Abigail feared that her friend's legs might give way. Sylvia Hafner was leading them towards Otto Kaufmann who, at that moment, stood alone, eyes still bright with after-performance excitement.

When they came to rest on Martina an even brighter light seemed to flash in them, and he took Martina's faintly shaking hand in his, almost forgetting, Abigail could swear, to return it to its owner.

Sylvia then introduced Abigail, but it was as though Martina's friend hardly existed for the young and brilliant pianist outside a polite smile and a nod. Martina's voice faltered at first as Otto began talking to her, then, to Abigail's relief, it returned to its normal tone and, she was to learn afterwards, from that moment the acquaintanceship never looked back.

Looking for Rolf, she felt a considerable jolt to her system when she saw that the woman to whom he was talking was only too familiar. All evening she had been rejoicing at the absence of the woman all the world, and, more important, the Felder family itself, called Rolf's girlfriend. Now she realised that it must have been the crush of people which had hidden Laura Marchant from her view.

And it must also have been Laura, she reflected, who had detained Rolf for so long before the concert had started. She had probably been the reason, also, for his disappearance from her side during the interval. Which meant, without doubt, that whenever Laura was around Rolf could not tear himself away from her.

Well, she reasoned, it was to be expected, wasn't it? Hadn't Laura, in her position as a financial journalist, done him an undeniable favour by warning him of the totally unexpected take-over bid for the Felder group of hotels? And on top of all that, wasn't she immensely attractive? What kind of weapons did Abigail Hailey possess, she asked herself unhappily, with which to fight such a formidable rival?

Rolf, deeply involved in his conversation, had made no effort to dislodge Laura's hand from his shoulder. Not only that, Abigail nodded, her heart sinking, he was holding the woman's gaze with his own. As he talked, Laura nodded, a half-smile playing over her face. Come back with me to my hotel, her eyes were inviting, and I guarantee you won't want to leave until morning.

As Rolf talked his eyes swept unseeingly around. It was as if nothing could distract his concentration — until his gaze alighted on Abigail. He paused in mid-sentence and stretched out his hand towards her.

Laura followed his eyes and her lips took on an unattractive pout. Her tactics changed and she moved to place herself between her companion and the object of his attention, but he moved, also, his mouth forming the word, 'Abigail.' He had raised his voice over the noise of the crowd, and his speaking of her name had held a note of command.

I *will not* dance to his tune, Abigail decided with a toss of her head. She looked around for Raymond, who moved across to her at once.

'Feeling lonely, Abby?' He nodded to Martina. 'She is well away. Her dream has come true, from the look

of things. See, Otto is writing down her address and
phone number. I wish——' he smiled sweetly at Abigail
'—I had his way with the ladies, but the lady I like so
much does not return my affection.'

He put his fingers over the protest she was about to
utter, then slid them down to rest on her shoulder.

'And my brother——' Raymond's mouth turned
down '—he is well away, too. That woman will get him
one day, I am certain. And so is Martina. The lady has
a formidable intellect, which matches his, and——' a
soundless whistle came from him '—what else besides,
eh? But she is not my type. I see you are trying not to
yawn, which means you're tired and want to go home.
Come with me in a cab. I'll take my brother's place
beside you, and he——' Raymond darted a defiant
glance at the man in question '—can go to hell. With
his lady friend.'

Raymond had left her at the door of her room. He had
seemed to have forgotten to let go of her hand. His
eyes had held a kind of muted longing, but he'd
released her hand at last.

'It's OK, I know when to go,' he'd said regretfully,
and with a sigh had left her.

Staring through the window, Abigail tried to make
out the line of the lake, imagining the dramatic backdrop of the mountains, and wondering whether Rolf
would manage to evade Laura Marchant's clutches and
make it back to the hotel that night. But don't fool
yourself, she thought with acerbity; what normal, virile
man would *want* to evade that woman's clutches?

Maybe, she thought, playing with the curtain's pull-
cord, he had needed no persuasion, but had willingly
accompanied the lady back to *her* hotel, with the
intention of staying there until dawn, and beyond.

Sighing, she jumped when the telephone rang. Refusing to move her legs in time with her racing heart, she
strolled to answer it. If it was Rolf—who else could it
be at that time of night?—he had to be made to

understand that she wouldn't always run at his beck and call.

'Hi,' said Martina, bubbling over.

OK, so settle down, Abigail told her heart.

'I just have to tell you. His sister——' Martina assumed that Abigail would know at once to whom the 'his' referred '——wants me to make some outfits for her. And guess what? I invited him to the house party. *And he accepted*. He said he was free on that date. Just as long, Otto said, as there was a piano on the premises, so that if he felt the need to escape from the merry throng he could, because he wasn't terribly good at parties. I assured him there was a piano—one of the best, too.'

'So it's "Otto" now, is it?' Abigail teased.

'He insisted. Oh, Abby, I'm on a high, I'm floating.'

'The only drug involved being love?' Abigail commented, laughing.

'We-ell, let's call it friendship at this stage, shall we? Friendship with fireworks. Oh, did I tell you? At the party we're having them. Fireworks, I mean. And my fashion show. Plus loads of food.'

'But most important of all, a well-known concert pianist called Otto Kaufmann, yes?'

'You are so right,' was Martina's laughing response. 'Night. But one thing we're not going to do,' she added with a laugh, 'is ask him to perform. We couldn't possibly afford his fee!'

It was as Abigail stepped out of the shower and reached for the towel that a movement behind her nearly made her jump out of her damp skin. She turned quickly.

'Rolf? Oh, Rolf, you frightened me. And—and. . .' She wrapped her arms around herself. 'I don't remember inviting you in here.'

'No?' He was holding the towel out of her reach. 'You are saying that omitting to lock your bathroom door was not an invitation?'

'I suppose,' she challenged, 'you broke the rules again and let yourself in.'

His smile was tight, his eyes busy appreciating the curves and inlets of her figure. 'You will have to complain to the management again, hmm? So complain, madam, complain. I am the management — a section of it.' His roving gaze was sending pinpoints of excitement chasing all over her. 'But I don't promise to give you a fair hearing.'

'I thought — I thought you'd be seeing your lady friend back to her place, ——'

He frowned. 'What lady friend? You're referring to Laura? And. . .and what? Staying the night?' His expression became a little cruel. 'Not when there are "pastures new", as they say, awaiting me on my own territory.'

'You think an awful lot of yourself, don't you?' she shot back, incensed. 'Not to mention of your own powers of attraction.' Which were, she was forced to admit, from her point of view powerful indeed.

His half-smile tantalised. He too, it seemed, had showered; she could tell by the dampness of his hair. His unfastened shirt, hanging loosely over his jeans, revealed a mat of chest hair straying down beyond his lean waist. He looked virile and alive and just a little reckless, with a kind of hunger in his eyes that set her skin tingling and burning and shivering all at once.

She *had* to resist him. If he went ahead and did with her exactly what it was plain he wanted to do, it would leave a mark on her life so indelible that she would never forget it.

'*Please*, Rolf.' A little desperately, she reached high to capture the towel, then realised just how much of herself she was revealing by the action, but he continued to torment her by holding it even higher.

'Tell me —— ' his eyes narrowed angrily ' — why did you not come to me when I called to you at the end of the concert?'

How could she tell him, I couldn't bear to be the unwanted third at what was so obviously a cosy tête-à-tête? Instead, she raised defiant eyes and told him, 'I don't have to come at your every call just because of this.' She raised the hand that bore his ring.

'Which, interpreted, means that you still like my brother's company better than mine? I saw you look round for him as if you couldn't spend another minute without him.'

That was desperation, she could have told him, not an overpowering desire for his company; desperation to find an excuse, any excuse, for not accepting your invitation at that moment.

'Do you, perhaps,' he pursued the subject relentlessly, 'prefer his goodnight kisses, his coaxing words and gentle persuasion to my rougher touch?'

'You're so wrong,' was all she could find to say, wishing with all her heart that her towelling robe was within easy reach.

Acutely aware of her undressed state, she swung round and groped instead for a face towel, anything to cover even a small part of her. He had guessed her intention and, tossing the bath-towel aside, seized her shoulders. Swinging her round and tugging her arms from across her body, he held her wrists wide apart, his eyes once again raking her figure, lingering on her breasts, then down, down, until the whole of her throbbing femininity came under his ruthless inspection.

'You—are—beautiful,' he said softly. She tried to free her wrists, but he tightened his hold. 'So shy? Surely a man has praised your naked beauty before?'

No man, she wanted to tell him, has ever been this close to me, seen me like this, not even Des Casey, my ex-boyfriend. She had liked Des a lot, and had told him so at the time, but not enough, she had discovered on thinking deeply about his constant demand that she should let him make love to her—real love, as he'd called it. Yes, he'd answered, he liked *her* a lot, too, but he had to be honest; he didn't *love* her, not in that kind of way.

'That,' she prevaricated now, her flushed face raised to Rolf's, 'would be telling.'

'Fencing with me, Miss Hailey? Dressed — or perhaps I should say undressed — as you are, that is dangerous.'

'Please, I want the towel.' Again she tried to break away, but he stopped her easily.

'Oh, no,' came from him huskily. 'I'm going to hold you. . .'

At the moment that he released her hands, she made a dive past him to grab the bath-towel, but his foot moved it further away. She tripped over the bath-mat and found herself sprawled at his feet — his bare feet, she saw with a shock.

'At last I have you,' he murmured, 'just where I want you.'

He crouched down and his palms stroked her back, moving slowly to her waist, then lower still, holding, probing, caressing. She gasped at his hands' audacity, twisting round and running her nails from his ankles to his toes. His quick, sharp breath should have warned her, but her nails dug deeper. He gripped her waist with both hands and turned her on to her back on the carpet.

'You want to play rough, *Liebling*? Suits me, lady. So do I.'

He came down on top of her, having shed his garments with a few lightning actions, and she felt the full arousal of him against the most sensitive areas of her body.

'I want you now, Abby,' he said thickly, raining kisses over her shoulders and back. 'There is no turning back from here. I have wanted you —— ' her ears caught the urgency in his voice ' — ever since I first set eyes on you, since I lifted you into my arms that day from the roadway where my car had thrown you.'

A shadow passed across his eyes at the memory of the pain he had unintentionally caused her.

'I know also,' he went on, 'and you cannot deny it, that you have wanted me. I have seen it in your eyes. And your integrity is such that you would not have accepted my ring, even though it was a gesture of convenience, if you had felt nothing for me.'

'Oh, God, Rolf, I. . .' Her breath was drawn on a gasp of pleasure and pain. 'We mustn't go on. I don't have any form of——'

'I will provide all the protection you need, my heart.'

But she wasn't his 'heart', she agonised; another woman was that. Hadn't he spent as much of the evening with her as possible? And hadn't he tolerated her possessive gestures towards him?

'It's still "no", Rolf.'

His hands gentled just a little. 'You want me to persuade you, to caress your consent from you? That's OK by me, Abby.'

'Rolf,' she protested, 'the floor——'

'Is hard? OK, so we will move.' He lifted her, wrapping her now pliant body around his waist. He paused, gazing with a hard, sensual stare into her eyes, before dropping her on to the bed and joining her there, rolling on to his side.

His eyes made free with every dip and hollow of her, then his mouth lowered to encompass the burgeoning mounds of her breasts, taking their peaks into his keeping, tugging, kissing, until she gasped with the pleasure and the agony of it.

He turned his attention to her stomach, following his trailing fingers with his lips, his tongue, moving lower until she writhed and cried out at their onslaught, the almost uncontrollable desire he was arousing within her.

'Touch me,' he growled, 'excite me, too, *Geliebte*. You know where.'

'Rolf,' she choked, 'I can't. . . I don't. . .'

He moved to stare into her wide eyes. 'No?' A second's pause, then, 'You need to be taught the language of love? I will teach you, Abby. Oh, yes, I will teach you. . .' He took her hand and she gasped again, never having known such abandonment, such intensity of sensation. Holding him so intimately aroused her to a pitch which was driving her beyond reason.

'Rolf, please. . .' Her mouth was dry, her throat parched.

'Please what, my own?' he teased huskily, tantalising her. 'You will have to spell it out for me.' His tongue ran around her ear, trailed her throat, and found its way yet again to her swollen breasts. 'Tell me what you want.'

'I want you, so take me,' she whispered hoarsely, 'make me yours. Oh, God, Rolf, I l. . .' *Love you!* More than that — adore you. I pledge myself to you. . . She closed her lips so that the give-away words could not escape.

He prised them open, taking over her mouth, then her body, shifting and making a pathway for himself inside her, and she almost cried at his gentleness and care. Then, abandoning all control, he moved and thrust and took her with him, breathing her tiny cries of pleasure into his own mouth until, rapturously, they reached a dazzling summit, then, after long, golden moments, joyously and together they descended breathless into peace and utter tranquillity.

He lay, his head on her breasts, still possessing her, the fires dying down. His eyes were brilliant as they found hers, and their gazes locked together as intricately as their bodies were still entangled.

'I guessed it might be so,' he murmured hoarsely, 'but never as good, as consummate, as this.' At length, he rolled from her. 'Now sleep, my heart. We must rest. This first time for you, I will not be greedy, although even now my body is hungering for you again.'

During the night he pulled her to him and, in her sleepy state, her responses were even more abandoned, and it was as though he could not have enough of her. Eventually, they slept, until the breeze billowed into the curtains, revealing the brilliant sunshine outside.

He half sat up and leaned over her. 'I want you again, Abby, but this time I will discipline my reflexes and stop them in their tracks. But as soon as circumstances allow I will come back to your bed and make love to you all over again. And——' he leaned down to kiss a wanton breast that somehow wriggled free of the bed cover '—we will spend the day together. . . Can you guess how, Abby?'

There was not a single part of her that did not leap in response to his words, let alone at the promise implicit within them. But it was an impossible dream.

His finger smoothed her brow. 'Why are you frowning?'

'Rolf. . .' It nearly killed her to say it. 'If this is the start of an affair——'

He had caught her frown. 'What if it is?'

'I don't want an affair with you.' Not without the love that should go with it, her mind continued, but she did not give voice to the words. Hadn't he told her at the beginning of their 'arrangement' that there would be no promise of love?

He swung his long legs to the floor, standing straight, totally masculine, looking down at her. He looked grim. 'Thanks for the memory, yes? And goodbye.'

His jaw moved and his hands found his hips. He looked so magnificent, in their new intimacy his hard muscularity provoking an immediate and overwhelming response from her feminine reflexes. She clenched her fists to prevent her body from springing up and begging for him to love her all over again.

'I think, Miss Hailey——' he leaned forward and swept her body free of covering, his brooding eyes raking every part of her '—that we will play it my way, not yours.'

He lifted her bodily and pushed through into the bathroom, sliding her acutely senitised skin through his palms to stand before him in the shower. He turned the water on and Abigail shrieked as it cascaded fast and furiously over her, soaking her hair before the rest of her. It pounded over him, too, but he disregarded it, pulling her to him. Their limbs entangled and it was only the ring of the telephone that prevented the lovemaking from starting all over again.

Abigail ran out of the shower, dripping water, to answer it.

'Who?' she asked. 'Herr Felder? You're back? I didn't know. Rolf?' She covered the mouthpiece, colouring deeply. 'Your father.' She held out the receiver.

A towel draped around his waist, he took the call. 'Father.' He listened. 'No, Raymond would not know where I was, nor Martina. And certainly not Reception.' He listened again. 'Oh, you guessed, did you?' he said with a half-smile. 'OK, so I'm here. And yes——' with a sleepy glance over his shoulder '—Abigail is here, too. Did she not answer the phone? But don't draw any conclusions from it, will you? I have it from her own lips that it is not the start of an affair. So why did you call?'

The conversation that followed was in their own language, and Abigail took herself back to the bathroom to dry herself and pull on a robe. As she tied the belt around her waist, the call ended.

'Rolf?' He seemed a little preoccupied. 'How did your father know you were here?'

'He rang my room, naturally, then Reception, who weren't able to help him. He even tried my apartment in Zurich. Then his imagination—aided by wishful thinking—took a great leap and he tried here. The renovators of the house—our family house—called him to say that their work was finished and that the place was ready for occupation just as soon as we had inspected it and passed it as satisfactory.'

'Does that mean bringing the house party forward?' Does it also mean, she longed to ask him, that my days with the Felder family, and especially with you, are numbered?

'Almost certainly. There will be no obstacle, either, to our moving in whenever we wish.' That 'our', she told herself with a silent sigh, naturally excluded herself.

He stretched hugely, the towel around him falling to the floor. His long arms lifted aloft, dark patches of hair revealing themselves all over him, and arousing her so erotically that she had to pretend to be looking for her slippers.

He came up behind her, wrapping her to him. 'Today I have work to do. It's not exactly onerous, nor will it take me long. It's not far from here and it will take me to a beauty spot.' He turned her between his hands. 'Would you like to come with me?'

Her heart leapt at the prospect of spending the day with him. 'I'd like that.'

'Good.' He pulled on his clothes, going to the door and glancing at his watch. 'One hour from now you will find me waiting for you at Reception.'

He lifted his hand and was gone.

If she had any regrets regarding what had happened between them — and she knew for certain that, beneath the surface of her mind, there were many waiting to pounce — then at that moment, and for that day, they would stay right where they were, disregarded and suppressed.

She had gone against the dictates of her reason and let her emotions lead the way — right into his enveloping, demanding arms. So what if she had followed her basic instincts blindly, even eagerly? She had those hours, at least, to remember him by, even if, in the years to come, those memories filled her with torment and longing.

CHAPTER NINE

ROLF and Abigail went up into the high hills in the post bus. The gradients were steep and the road twisted and turned, the hairpin bends being breath-robbing and seemingly impossible for the long vehicle to cope with. At each bend the post horn was sounded loud and clear, its varied notes musical and pleasant on the ear, but a dire warning to any oncoming vehicle.

Abigail, seated beside Rolf, dreaded the moment when that might happen. When a car did approach, descending towards them, she held her breath, putting her hand to her mouth. Rolf laughed, taking that hand into his keeping.

'The driver is very experienced,' he assured her. 'See, he's reversing into this bay and the oncoming car is going past.'

Abigail looked down, then closed her eyes quickly at the steep drop which fell away from the road on her side of the bus, which, its engine ticking over as if panting with its exertions, made it to the passing bay and waited patiently.

Even as they resumed the ascent the mist persisted, but it did not hide the great variety of colourful flowers growing by the roadside. Owners of the houses *en route* had stocked up for the winter with piles of logs. Rakes leant against walls. These were intended, Rolf explained, for the women in the family to use during the haymaking season.

Reaching the top at last, they emerged from the bus into an immensely rural scene. The mist had not lifted for the entire journey. It veiled, but did not conceal, the great sweeping hills and, beyond them, the line of rugged mountains.

'It's beautiful,' Abigail exclaimed. 'It's different from anything I've seen so far. It's pastoral; that's the best

way I can think of to describe it. It makes music, you
know?' She glanced up at Rolf, whose face held a smile
she could not interpret. 'You're proud of your country,
aren't you?' she commented.

'Who wouldn't be?' was all he said, the sweep of his
arm saying the rest.

Everywhere she looked, Abigail saw the land rising
and rising again, slope on slope, each hill being dwarfed
by a more distant and even grander incline. In the
distance, the sun shone, catching high peaks and giving
them brightness and colour.

Near by, trees climbed the hills, their roots deep in
the varied greens of the meadow grass. There were
paths everywhere, criss-crossing and leading to isolated
farms and houses.

They walked for a while, coming to a halt when Rolf
pointed out the city below them that they had left
behind. Red roofs were scattered all over the valley,
climbing the lower hills, bordering roads so far below
that they seemed like pencil drawings.

Descending a steep slope, they found a road that led
through a valley. All around, cowbells rang, their tones
varied, the cattle that bore them contentedly munching
the lush grass.

Abigail paused beside a barn where posters were
displayed. 'Could you translate what these are saying?'
she asked.

Rolf obliged. 'They're certificates of merit. They've
been put there by proud dairy farmers who own the
cattle which have won prizes in competitions.' He began
to lead the way back. 'I have someone I must see.
Come.' He held out his hand. 'Are you hungry?'

'A little.' She looked about her, wondering where
Rolf had it in mind to eat.

They approached a café, built mainly of wood, but
with a red-tiled roof. He led her into the open-air
section and seated her at a table, putting a menu into
her hand.

'Ten minutes, and my business will be finished.'

He was absent for longer, and Abigail recalled the

time when he had taken her on the rack-and-pinion train to the top of a mountain. He had disappeared into the hotel's interior on that occasion.

She smiled with relief when he emerged at last.

'Have you bought this café, too?' she asked, with a mischievous smile.

'Ah, you remember the last time I took you into the mountains.' He smiled, seating himself beside her. 'And the answer is, probably, yes.'

She laughed. 'Do you spend your time buying up these places and adding them to the Felder group?'

'On occasion. I make preliminary enquiries, that's all. My heart is with my own engineering company in Zurich.'

And that, she thought, is where it will stay. Hadn't Raymond warned her? A workaholic, he had described his brother as. No room in his life — no *permanent* room — for any member of the opposite sex. Remember that, her reasoning self reminded her. But her emotions, still heated from Rolf's lovemaking, told it to be silent and to stop trying to spoil this wonderful day.

Abigail opted for a light meal, followed by coffee. The waitress, hearing them speak in English, followed suit.

'Where are you from?' Abigail enquired of the young woman.

'I am from Holland.'

'But your English is so good, I really thought you came from there.'

'Now that is a nice compliment.' Rolf addressed the waitress. 'Do you live here now?'

'Only temporarily. I have an upstairs room in the café. Soon I'm going back home. I am to be married.'

'How wonderful,' Abigail commented, then heard with dismay the pleasure in her own voice. How had Rolf taken it? As a reproach to him for not offering her a commitment, which she knew from Raymond that he had forsworn anyway? A secret glance at his face told her nothing.

'Which means,' Rolf commented to the waitress, 'that there will be a vacancy here?' She nodded. 'Has it been advertised yet?'

'It will be, as soon as I know the exact date when I'll be leaving here.'

Rolf, businessman now, despite his relaxed manner and casual clothes, nodded. If the Felder Group was, as he had hinted, interested in purchasing the business, then the replacement of an employee, Abigail surmised, would be a matter of interest to him.

A group of young men entered noisily, spreading themselves around the vacant tables, legs flung out, manner jovial. They were in uniform, grey in colour with shoulder tabs and brown belts around the waist, their peaked caps set jauntily. Noticing Abigail's interest, they removed their caps to the accompaniment of sweeping bows.

Abigail coloured and touched Rolf's hand, her eyes questioning. He turned in his seat, taking note of the young men's interest in his companion. His frown held thunder and they subsided surprisingly quickly at the 'hands off' sign.

'Soldiers — temporary, but well trained,' he informed Abigail. He turned to them again, speaking in German. They nodded, seizing menus.

'They say they have just completed their period of military training. It takes place around here. This is something we have to do in my country.'

'But—' Abigail frowned '—you're a neutral nation.'

'That's so, but we are ready should anybody threaten us. You understand? After our initial basic training, we have to repeat that training periodically.' A glance at his watch indicated that his mind was moving on. Her day with him, her wonderful day, she became ruefully aware, was drawing to a close. He told her where the ladies' room could be found.

He rose with her. 'I have to make a phone call. I'll see you back here. It shouldn't take me long.'

She was seated and waiting, however, some time

before he returned. Her mood had undergone a sea
change. Although the sun shone just as brightly, she
could have sworn there were many more clouds in the
sky. On looking up, she saw that the sky was in fact
cloudless. It was in her heart that there was a painful
dullness.

She knew why her thoughts were playing tricks. She
had heard Rolf speaking on the telephone inside the
café — and he was speaking in his own language. Perfectly natural, she had thought — until she'd heard him
speak the name of the person to whom he was talking. . . Laura.

There had been no doubt about it. Laura Marchant,
the lady who, she was certain now, would one day win
his heart. She held all the aces, didn't she? Abigail
argued silently. The thing that had shaken her to the
core was the fact that the lady could speak Rolf's
language, not just metaphorically, but literally!

How could he resist her for long? Abigail pondered
in quiet desperation, tied up as Laura was in his
business affairs? She obviously had the specialised
knowledge which enabled her to give Rolf Felder, the
businessman, eagerly accepted advice. And she also
possessed the ability and the sophistication, didn't she,
to satisfy his needs in other, more intimate, respects?

The soldiers, who had merely had a snack and a
drink, rose from their tables, scraping back their chairs.
They paused beside Abigail.

Smiling and sweeping off their caps again, they spoke
in their own language, and she could only look from
one to the other, managing to smile, hoping she was
not offending them by doing so. They must have sensed
Rolf's presence behind them, since they nodded and
walked away, seemingly casual, but with feet that
moved quite fast, no doubt hoping to escape from his
possessive anger.

'What were they saying?' Abigail asked, looking up
at him as he towered over her.

'They were very poetic,' he observed curtly. 'They

were telling you that your eyes are like a blue sky with clouds lurking in the distance.'

This translation shook her. Had their recent training, she thought with wry amusement, turned them into mind-readers, not to say crystal-gazers?

'One of them also said that he was more than ready for a lady's softening influence after those stark weeks without their company, and please could he have a date with you. You can blush, Miss Hailey——' his hard fingers forced up her chin '—yet are you sure you gave them no encouragement?'

She shook her head free and sprang to her feet. 'You can't be serious. All I did when they arrived was look at them and wonder what they were doing here.'

Head in the air, she swept towards the entrance, leaving him behind. To her chagrin, she had to pause until he caught up with her, since she did not know which direction to take.

'OK, OK.' He grasped her wrist. 'Calm down.'

As he swung her to face him, the bus climbed the hill and sat waiting.

'After last night——' he began, but she broke in, the memory of his discussion with his lady friend still tearing at her heart.

'After last night, don't think you *own* me, Herr Felder. For me, as for you, it was a one-night stand.'

He threw her wrist away and strode towards the bus, standing back with icy politeness for her to board it ahead of him. During the return journey, it was as if they were two strangers whom chance had brought together to share the same seat.

At least we're quits, Abigail thought, swallowing her tears. But the basis of her desire for revenge had been jealousy, pure and simple, and it was tearing her apart.

Abigail was working in the office, Anton Felder having, on his return, presented her with another pile of notes, when the telephone rang.

Her heart jumped but she told it not to be stupid. How could it be Rolf when he had flown to Frankfurt on business? He would be away for a few days, he had told her on leaving her two days ago at the end of their day together. They had returned from their outing into the hills in studied silence.

As he had waited with her for the lift, seeing her into it, she had blurted out, bitterness driving her against her better judgement, 'I suppose you're taking Laura Marchant with you?'

'You suppose right,' had been his cool response.

She could have cried with pain. Had those arms now folded across his chest, she agonised, really held her so closely last night? And had those lips, now set in a formidable line, truly kissed and caressed her with such passion?

The doors had begun to slide together. 'I hope you enjoy your sojourn with your lady friend,' Abigail had got out just before they closed, cutting him off from her sight.

'The dress I promised you,' Martina was saying now, 'for you to wear at the house-warming party — it's ready to be tried on. Can you spare the time?'

'Right now?' Abigail asked.

'As long as the work you're doing isn't urgent.'

Abigail assured her that it wasn't and took herself down to her friend's work-room.

'Your face is so long, Abby,' Martina exclaimed. 'What's eating you, for heaven's sake? Is it something my brother said?'

'Which brother?' Abigail asked with assumed innocence.

'Well, it's not Raymond, that's for sure,' Martina answered. 'Am I right?'

'Maybe, maybe not,' Abigail prevaricated, searching inside herself for a smile.

'That's better,' Martina commented. 'Everybody. . .' The three other women working there looked up. 'This is my friend, Abby.'

The young women nodded. Two of them were modelling outfits that clearly bore the Martina look.

The other, Liliane, lifted a hand from her sewing, saying, 'Hi.'

The rack of garments to be displayed at the dress show had been uncovered, but in a corner an intriguing conical shape stood hidden under layers of tissue.

Abigail, with Martina's help, donned the garment she had been summoned to try on. Studying her reflection, she gasped at how much of her the scarlet dress did not cover.

'It's a one-shoulder design,' Martina explained, fussily adjusting the sleeveless neckline, which slanted at an alarming angle from the single shoulder strap to a point well below the opposite armpit.

'Oh, please tighten it,' Abigail urged. 'Otherwise I'm sure it will slip down, and then heaven knows what it will reveal.'

Martina grinned impishly. 'You're referring to your bosom, of course. I'm sorry, but I won't tighten it. It will keep the men guessing all evening. You know, a kind of "will it, won't it, slip?" line of thought. But it won't. It's cut too neatly for that to happen.'

'It's great,' Abigail said, admiring the sparkle, the cut, the drape to the waist, the perfect fit from there over her hips to her calves, 'but Martina, I couldn't, I just couldn't.'

'You can and you will,' declared Martina, a feminine version of her elder brother at that moment, Abigail decided, if there ever was one. 'You cannot refuse it. You see, it's a gift from me. OK?'

'OK,' agreed Abigail, capitulating with a smile.

As she made for the door Martina said, 'This afternoon Raymond and I are driving to the house to make sure it has been cleared thoroughly and that everything is OK for the house-warming on Saturday. Would you like to come with us?'

Abigail thought of the pile of notes awaiting her attention.

Martina must have read her thoughts. 'Nothing urgent about your work, you said.'

'I'd love to, thanks.' Anything, she decided, as she

134

returned to the office, to take her mind off the thought of Laura Marchant enticing Rolf into her room, and her bed, every night.

Raymond drove them to the house. They climbed a hill to a line of trees, turning in through gates that led to a steep driveway.

The house was large, as Abigail supposed it would have to be to accommodate the Felder family. Its walls were painted white, its roof red-tiled with an overhang that acted as a cover for the wooden-railed balconies below it.

'Enter,' invited Martina as her brother used the key, then sniffed at the air. 'Paint, varnish and the smell of new carpets.'

'Oh, and flowers,' Abigail offered, 'masses of them!'

Martina nodded. 'The florists have certainly been busy. We employed them to do the floral honours for the house-warming party.'

The thick pile of the fabulous carpets softened the pressure of feet, and where the furnishings were concerned plainly no expense had been spared. The whiteness of the kitchen dazzled; its worktops and the utensils spread around it showed signs of having already been used.

'The caterers have been busy, too,' Martina observed, 'making preparations for the big day.'

The view from the main living area, with its floor-to-ceiling windows, had Abigail's eyes riveted. It was similar to the view from her hotel room, she decided, yet not quite the same, probably because the angle from which she looked at it was different. The ferry boats criss-crossed the rippling surface, the mountains rose just as majestically, but the wooded areas were nearer, the environs more rural and peaceful.

I could live here, Abigail thought, then closed her mind at once on the impossible dream.

Immediately below was the sloping land belonging to the property. It stretched into the distance, and only the lake itself seemed to halt its descent.

'Down there on the lakeshore is our boat-house,' Raymond explained. 'The small building near it is where our housekeeper and her husband live.'

'When I knew you in London,' she remarked with a smile, 'I had no idea that your background was so — so lavish, so rich in creature comforts.'

'I seemed like just an ordinary guy, yes? I'll tell you a secret, Abby. I am an ordinary guy. If you pinch me, I'll yell.'

'But the whole family, it's —'

'Rolling in money, as they say? You don't mean you object! You really should be framed and hung on the wall of my brother's room as an example of the female of the species who isn't, as he claims, out solely for money and position, but runs the other way.'

Please tell your brother that, she almost pleaded, but managed a smile instead.

'It's great, it's absolutely fantastic,' Martina declared, sweeping into the room. 'The whole place is spotless and ready for occupation. Tomorrow, Raymond, we must pack our belongings, and in three days' time we can move in.'

Oh, no, as soon as that? Abigail thought. If the family leaves the hotel, I must, too.

'I'll book a flight,' Abigail stated as matter-of-factly as she could manage.

Martina looked mystified. 'Where to? It's only a car ride from the Hotel Panorama Grand,' she joked.

'Home,' Abigail stated. 'Where else?'

'Home? You mean back to your own country? But there's room for you right here at this house. Raymond —' his sister turned to him ' — use your persuasive techniques. It works on most girls you get friendly with.'

'Not this one,' he averred, his eyes on the pattern of the carpet.

'Ah. I have the wrong brother, yes? Right.' She picked up the telephone which stood on a coffee-table. 'I will call my big brother. Maybe. . .' Her eyebrows rose, implying all kinds of things, and Abigail cursed the give-away colour, reflecting that Martina was not so absorbed by her work that she did not notice the changes in other people as a result of their experiences. 'Maybe it's Rolf's persuasive techniques that are called for. I know the number of the office he rents in Frankfurt.'

'Hi, Rolf?' She listened with a frown, then covered the mouthpiece, baring her teeth and growling, 'Gr-rr. Rolf's female hanger-on is speaking in German. She thinks she's so clever. Well, one day soon she'll realise she's been just a little too clever. Hi, Laura,' she said, continuing the call. 'It's OK. As you know very well, I can speak your language. There's no need to sh——' she mouthed the words 'show off', but managed to suppress them '—address me as if I were a cultural and linguistic moron. Yes, I would like to speak to my brother, please.'

Abigail was glad that the sinking of her heart could not be seen, but sink it did, as low as it could get. Well, Rolf had been honest with her, hadn't he, and admitted that Laura was accompanying him?

'Rolf?' Martina said. 'Raymond and I are at the house. It's ready and waiting for us to move in. But your *friend*, Abigail—yes, she is proving obstinate. She is refusing to join us here. You just have to persuade her to change her mind. Here she is.' She passed the receiver over.

'Abigail?' Why, she wondered, did he sound so angry? If she returned home, it would get her out of his way, wouldn't it? 'Is it true what my sister tells me?'

'I'm booking a flight home,' she confirmed flatly. 'Why? Because I'm not part of the Felder family.' Merely a female, she just prevented herself from adding, whom you use now and then to satisfy your male appetite. 'And that excludes me, doesn't it, from what is entirely a family affair?'

'Are you really trying to provoke me?' came through tight lips. 'There is a guest room available—more than one. And a smaller room which you can use as an office. In any case, there is the promise you made to help my father.'

'P-promise?' she cried. No promise of love, he'd said when he had slipped his mother's ring on her hand. How that hurt now, how the knife twisted in the wound. . .after all that had happened between them. 'You can talk of *promises*, when. . .?' A sob caught her by surprise.

She flung down the receiver, cutting the call, unable to stem the tears. Raymond cursed in his own language and Abigail felt his arms come round her. It was the wrong Felder brother, but what did it matter? she reasoned. He was offering comfort and sympathy, qualities which Rolf did not seem to possess.

'I h-hate him,' Abigail muttered thickly into Raymond's shoulder. 'He's pigheaded and unfeeling and selfish and—and he thinks only of himself.'

All the pent-up misery she had been feeling since their silent quarrel on the day of their outing came pouring out. It was some time before the crying stopped and Abigail finally dried her tears.

'That woman, that Laura,' Martina muttered, agitatedly plumping up cushions as if she were punching an invisible presence. 'Somehow I'll get her out of Rolf's life. And I have thought of a way. Watch out, Laura Marchant. I am Martina Felder, well-known fabric designer and established leader of fashion—even if I am for the moment known only in my own country. Miss Marchant, who, if I have anything to do with it, will never become Frau Rolf Felder, here I come.'

Three days later, their belongings packed and ready for removal to the house, Raymond ordered a late evening meal in the hotel restaurant, inviting Abigail to join him.

She accepted with some reluctance. Her appetite had unaccountably deserted her lately. She would really have preferred to spend the evening alone, perhaps taking a stroll along the lakeside.

Her thoughts would insist on returning time and

again to the night she had shared with Rolf. If she closed her eyes she could feel his lips on hers, imagine his erotic kisses on her heated skin, daydream that his arms were around her and hers around him.

As they strolled towards the exit of the now empty restaurant, Raymond drew her attention to the piano. Abigail touched the dark polished wood lovingly and played a note or two.

'Go ahead, I know you're itching to try it out,' Raymond encouraged. 'You never know, you might even sound as good as Martina's friend, Otto.'

Abigail smilingly shook her head, but took him up on his suggestion, seating herself and adjusting the height of the piano stool.

'Know where my sister's gone this evening?' Raymond asked as she did so.

'I saw her race out of the door waving a piece of paper,' Abigail told him. 'She seemed excited.'

'She was. That "piece of paper" was a ticket, a free one given to her by guess who? That's right, Otto Kaufmann. He was at the house when Martina visited his sister to give her a fitting for an outfit she's making for her.' He gestured. 'Make music, Abby.'

Her fingers ran over the keys as she sought in her mind for sounds to suit her mood. The tunes her hands produced were mellow and just a little sad, love-songs and romantic mood music that brought to her mind memories that were bright and clear, joyful and abandoned. . .yet filled with anguish and pain.

As she played, her eyes lifted to Raymond's face and by a strange trick of the light she saw not Raymond, but Raymond's brother. He was not smiling. Instead, his expression was aloof and full of rebuke. His eyes burned, not with love and passion, but with reproach and something like anger.

Her eyes shifted a little and her fingers slowed to a stop, the melody hanging on the air. She had not imagined him; he was there, a short distance from her, hands in pockets, lips a tight line.

Oh, God, she thought, he's convinced I was playing

for Raymond, that he was the object of my thoughts, when all the time I was thinking of you, Rolf Felder, seeing you in your brother's face, Rolf Felder. I love you, Rolf Felder. . .

'Hi.' Raymond's greeting broke the spell, but it did nothing to improve his brother's mood.

Raymond's eyes darted from Rolf to Abigail. He could not have missed the anger in his brother's face, nor Abigail's trembling lips. He must have correctly interpreted the movement of her throat as she swallowed the threatening tears.

'My wanderer brother is back at last. Rolf——' he swung to face him as Abigail closed the piano lid but remained seated, her hands clasped tightly on her lap '—would you like to know what my girlfriend called you?'

'Raymond, don't.' The choked appeal did not check him. 'I've never been——'

Raymond wasn't listening. 'She says you're selfish and pigheaded and unfeeling. Also, you think only of yourself. Now how do you like that as a character reference?'

'Please. I didn't mean it. I was upset at the time and——'

'She'd just talked to you on the phone.' Raymond seemed to be in his element. 'You made her cry, do you know that? And who was it who comforted her? Why, I did, your little brother, right here.' He patted his shoulder and grew strangely belligerent. 'I met her first, Rolf. She's *my* friend. My girlfriend. You understand?'

'Raymond.' Rolf spoke at last. '*Little* brother. You're too late. Did she not tell you? She's mine.'

'Abigail?' he queried unbelievingly. 'He's wrong, yes?' There was a long pause when Abigail could only gaze at him. 'So he's not wrong.' He began to walk away, then, as if he could not contain himself any longer, he swung back, fist raised, thrusting towards Rolf's chin. 'Why, you——'

'No!' The cry escaped Abigail's control.

'It's OK.' Raymond's fist deliberately swung wide of his brother's unmoving figure. 'I wouldn't hit him. You know——' his voice faltered a little '—I still look up to him and love him, even though he's done his abysmal, miserable worst to the girl I've wanted ever since I met her. But. . . I'll never forgive him.' He made to leave, but paused again. 'I warned you, Abby, not to trust him. Now it's too late.'

CHAPTER TEN

ABIGAIL, with Liliane's expert assistance, had helped Martina pack the precious contents of her work-room. It had taken some hours for the chaos that customarily reigned in Martina's busily creative world to be tamed and folded and coaxed into boxes and cases for transport to her new working area at the house.

Now they were there, in the basement of the house, unpacking and arranging and following Martina's instructions to the letter. Any deviation from them she would not tolerate. Raymond, poking his head round the door and listening to her decisive tones, had called her a hard taskmaster — or mistress, as he had corrected himself — and told her to remember that her helpers were volunteers, one of them unpaid.

The task accomplished at last, Martina came down to earth and thanked those helpers. Liliane protested that she was only doing her job. Abigail said that it was the least *she* could do in view of Martina's generosity in giving her couture-style clothes without charge.

The unpacking was almost finished, one item only remaining in its wrappers. Abigail had removed a layer of the pinned tissue paper, discovering beneath it a section of white satin and lace.

'What's this lovely thing?' she asked Martina. 'It positively glows. Is it a secret, or. . .'

'No, please.' Martina hurried over. 'It must remain covered. Although you're my friend, I'm not letting you into its secret,' she finished bluntly. 'Now how are you getting on with settling into your own room? Want any help? No? So come with me and view my father's suite, not to mention Rolf's. Mine you've seen already.'

Trailing behind her, Abigail climbed the staircase to the entrance floor, then climbed again to the first landing. Anton Felder's living space was large and comfortable and self-contained.

'And here's my elder brother's.' Martina swung the door wide.

The living-room was light and roomy, with modern upholstered furniture without frills or fancy touches.

'The sofa's made up in module style,' Martina commented. 'The paintings are splashes of colour and little else.' She shrugged. 'It's modern, it's OK, but it could do with some softening touches. It's Rolf's taste, but it's so practical; to me it even borders on the stark. It lacks a woman's touch, don't you think? And I don't mean his current lady friend's. The bedroom's the same — all one colour, cream. Unimaginative,' was her dismissing concluding comment.

It was the view that drew Abigail's eyes, similar to her own, except that the lake seemed to sparkle more brightly, the mountains seeming even grander and more majestic.

The telephone rang in the living area. Martina answered. 'Hi, Raymond.' She listened. 'He is? Then we'd better scatter pronto. Thanks for the warning.'

'Come.' She beckoned. 'Elder brother is on his way up here, Raymond said. He's just met the sibling in question down in the entrance hall.'

She was in the corridor, but it seemed they had not moved quickly enough. 'Hi, Rolf,' she said in a loud voice, as if giving a signal, but Abigail did not have time even to make it through the door.

Rolf loomed large in the doorway, eyes on Abigail. 'Stay here,' he directed, adding a belated, 'Please.'

'Bye, Abby,' Martina called. 'Sorry, but I'm making my getaway fast. Thanks a million for your help.'

Rolf closed the door behind him. His mood seemed so dark that Abigail wished she had been able to make her escape as Martina had done.

'What — what do you want?' Abigail's feet took her backwards before she could stop them. 'Why should I stay?'

She felt the impact of him as if he were a force-ten

gale. He took her breath away just by standing there, hands in business-jacket pockets, legs slightly, almost threateningly, apart. His dark brows were drawn together, his eyes holding a wintry light.

A muscle worked in his jaw. 'You're in my territory. You have put your head in my noose.'

Her blood went cold at the implication in his words, but she managed a smile. 'You—you don't have to tighten it, do you?'

He was not moved by her attempt to humour him.

'It's been bugging me. And don't pretend you don't know what I'm talking about.' Two slow steps brought him nearer. 'I'm pigheaded, am I? Unfeeling? Selfish? Why are you shaking your head? Did you, or didn't you, make those accusations against my character?'

She had to be truthful. 'I did. But Rolf, I——'

'You did. That's all I wanted to know.' His hand went to his pocket. 'Selfish, you said. That cut me deeply. I had to prove otherwise, to clear my character in that respect, at least. So I've bought you a present. Will you give me your wrist.' It was an order, not a question.

'Why?'

'Why? There is something I want to place around it.'

He withdrew a box from his pocket. It was oblong in shape. The gold watch he lifted from its dark velvet lining glowed in the afternoon light.

Abigail could not suppress a gasp. 'But why?'

'Why not? You're a very. . .beautiful lady.'

'No, I'm not.' She shook her head wildly, then rebuked herself for acting so foolishly.

'You want me to tell you so in a more, shall we say, romantic way?' He took her wrist, fixing the watch into place.

She saw the four diamonds inset into the amber face, one diamond for each quarter of the hour. She read the name, and it registered that it was one of the famous brands she had seen advertised in bright lights over the city's numerous jewellers' shops.

'It must have cost a small fortune. I. . .' She pushed
back her hair. 'I can't accept it, Rolf.'

He held her eyes for some seconds, hers dropping
first. Slowly he removed his jacket, tossing it aside, his
eyes never moving from her.

'It's beautiful, Rolf. . .' Give it back, a voice was
urging; you mustn't accept it. She moistened her lips to
repeat her refusal of it, but the words wouldn't come.

'So overcome your scruples and keep it,' he stated
with decision. 'Does it prove that at least one of your
accusations is wrong? That I am at least not selfish?'
His voice had softened. He moved and she held her
breath. 'Abigail.' His hands rested on her shoulders,
sliding down to her elbows and her hands, opening her
arms wide, in a gesture that had her blushing at the
memory of the other time he had done such a thing.
Then, as now, his narrowed gaze had raked her, taking
in every detail of her shape and womanliness.
'Abby. . .' It came in a mere whisper.

With impatient palms he pushed at her cotton top
until it lifted over her head and fell to the floor. Then
his arms were round her, robbing her of breath, his
chest compressing her breasts.

'Know something, *Liebling*?' His lips skimmed her
bare shoulder. 'I have thought about you all the time
I've been away.'

She twisted her head to stare up at him. 'How can
you say that,' she asked, 'when I know for certain that
Laura Marchant was with you?'

A little of his anger returned. 'Will you leave Laura
out of this?' His hands easily stilled her efforts to get
away from him. He gathered her wrists together behind
her and with them eased her backwards. She gasped,
fearing she would lose her balance. His mouth
descended, closing over her parted lips, intruding,
tasting, savouring her mouth's every hollow, until her
legs threatened to give way under her.

He released her wrists and impelled her upwards,
and of their own accord her arms closed around his

neck. He swept her up and pushed at a door, swinging her on to his bed.

He paused to divest himself of his shirt, throwing it aside, doing likewise to her bra. Her eyes urged her lips to press against his muscled torso, and she followed their instructions, nuzzling her face against the wiry whorls across his chest.

Was it too much to ask, she thought mistily, that he was beginning to need her as much as she needed him? Was there more than mere desire in his lovemaking? He had thought about her, he'd said, but had emotion been mixed in with his very male drive that had caused him to think about her?

Then her memory jolted her thoughts back on to the rails from which they had almost jumped. He had taken Laura with him. Surely she would have fulfilled his masculine longings? Which had to mean that he was merely bluffing when he'd told her just now how much he had thought of her while he'd been away.

'Rolf,' she choked, 'I don't want——'

'Don't lie.' His voice was muffled. 'You do.'

'No, I. . .' It was no use, she just couldn't force herself to resist.

He was kissing her now, in her most vulnerable places, and she was writhing under the caress of his lips as they wandered to all kinds of areas which he knew, by experience — the thought made her blush — aroused her deeply.

Get away from him, her saner self was urging; dislodge those arrogant lips of his from their seductive safari all over you. Its infinitely reasonable advice was lost in the rising tide of joy that was sweeping her at being back where for all the days of his absence she had longed to be.

Her arms lifted high in her ecstasy as his mouth closed erotically over the hard pink centre of her breasts. . .and her fevered gaze caught the glint of the late afternoon sun on the diamonds in the watch he had just given her. And it came to her like the flash of distant lightning why he had given her such a lavishly expensive gift. . .

With all the strength she could dredge from her compliant, intoxicated body, she pushed at his shoulders, his chest, anywhere that her hands could find on his powerful person to dislodge him from her.

At last her intention got through to him and he lifted his head, eyes narrow, staring at her face.

'What's wrong?' he grated. 'Are you trying to tell me something? Like, I'm the wrong man? The right surname, perhaps, but the wrong brother?'

'Don't be silly, Rolf, it's——'

He lifted himself from her, standing, hands on hips, beside the bed. 'Silly now, am I? I have to add that, do I, to the list of the negative characteristics that you've drawn up about me? Who are you trying to fool, Abigail?' He was drawing on his shirt, buttoning it one-handedly. 'I caught you off guard when I arrived unexpectedly the other evening as you played the piano at the hotel.' He tucked his shirt inside his trousers and refastened the zip. 'You were gazing into Raymond's face as if he were the love of your life.'

'You're wrong,' she cried, swinging her legs and sitting on the side of the bed. 'I was. . .' How could she tell him? I was seeing you in his face; he's like you, yet he's not, so in my dream-like state I superimposed your face on to his, and I was playing my heart out—for you? He wouldn't believe her, would he?

She picked up her bra and fixed it under his slightly insolent gaze. Then she retrieved her cotton top and pulled it over her head.

Her face emerged to challenge him. 'How can you speak so self-righteously about my fantasising about someone else—that's what you meant, wasn't it?—when all the time you were making love to me *you* were pretending it was someone else?'

A moment's pause, but her heart sank when he did not dispute her statement; then, standing and facing him, she accused, 'I know why you gave me this watch.'

'I told you why,' was his cold response.

'Ah, but that wasn't the truth. Tell me honestly; it was to prove a point, wasn't it? To prove to yourself how right you are—have been, in fact, ever since the lady in your past, called Beatrice, deserted you for a millionaire—that all that women want from life is wealth and position, with the emphasis on wealth.'

'So?' His dark brows arched. Once again he made no attempt to deny her accusation, and she wept inside.

'So, after our—our recent night together——' passionate, unforgettable, a small voice added '—you thought you'd test me by buying something that cost a small fortune, with its gold and its diamonds, and presenting it to me under the guise of persuading me you were truly a generous and thoughtful person. Which, if I accepted it, would justify and reinforce your assertion that all women were gold-diggers and out only for themselves. Well——' she removed the watch from her wrist and held it out to him '—you can put it back in its box.' Head high, she held his unreadable gaze. 'Thank you for the thought. I hope I'm now proving to you that there's one woman in the world at least who cannot be parted from her principles. You can keep your wealth; you can keep your position.' At the door, she swung round. 'Y-you can k-keep your lovemaking for the real woman in your life, the one you took with you to Frankfurt.'

'Abigail.' Somehow he was there in front of her. 'So think that of me.' A shrug, then his arms went round her, so tightly that her head drooped back. She closed her eyes, fighting her instincts, fighting her body, which ached for him, for the way he was kissing her at that moment, her throat, her mouth, which had placed itself so as to catch his as it ascended.

A sob escaped her as she tugged herself free. She was addicted to this man, and nothing but ruthless denial on her part would get him out of her system.

'I'm sorry, Rolf,' she whispered hoarsely. 'I know now you don't trust me. So it's no.'

A glance told her of his anger, but she forced her

feet to take her from him. Just in time she made it to her room. She couldn't hold back the tears a moment longer.

'So you made the journey from the hotel to the grand Felder residence?'

Anton's eyes twinkled as Abigail glanced up, smiling, from the desk in the small room that had been designated her private office.

'It was a shorter journey, yes,' he went on, 'than the one which would have taken you home?'

Abigail was puzzled. 'How did you know, Herr Felder, that I was thinking of returning home?'

'My elder son asked me to try and change your mind, should he and his sister and brother fail. I would have been very upset to lose my very efficient assistant. Already I feel I haven't thanked you enough for all you've done. And please —— ' his hand rested briefly on her shoulder ' — don't run away from here yet, will you? There are plenty more where those notes have come from.'

He looked at her hand poised over the keys. 'Ah,' he said with undoubted satisfaction, 'you are still wearing the ring my son gave you.'

'Yes, but —— ' his glad smile worried her ' — all the family knows why it's there. It has no significance beyond that. Rolf and I, we mean nothing to each other. We. . .' Her voice threatened to crack, so she stopped, hoping he would not question her further.

A look of deep compassion met her upward glance. How much had this warmly sympathetic man guessed? Had the look in her eyes given her away?

'Rolf is a busy man,' Anton offered vaguely. 'He's away again. He returns tomorrow, hopefully, in time for the party. You are coming? Of course you are. You will celebrate with us that we have a home of our own for the first time for years. You like the house?'

'It's wonderful.'

'You could live here?'

With Rolf beside me, I could live here forever, she thought, but answered, 'Easily.'

He nodded and reached into his briefcase, extracting a folder. 'More notes, my dear.' He placed them on the desk. 'I really am grateful. Now I must supervise the preparations. Martina told me she would do it, but she's so busy with her collection of clothes, I doubt if she'll have the time. And Raymond——' he smiled fondly ' — he is just Raymond.' Lifting a hand, he went on his way.

Rolf had not returned by the following morning. If the weather held, Martina had told her, the party would be held on the terrace. If not, then in the house.

The weather did hold, and from sunrise onwards there was a breathless kind of activity in the house, emanating from the kitchen outwards. Florists came to put the finishing touches to their lavish arrangements. Electricians erected poles along each side of the terrace, to which they fixed strings of multi-coloured lights.

Loudspeakers appeared at every corner. Glass doors were flung wide; long tables, covered by brilliantly white cloths, held a promise of food which begged to be consumed, along with bottles of every kind of drink imaginable.

'All this must have cost a fortune,' Abigail commented to Martina when she emerged, flushed and a little bothered, from her work-room, to keep her promise, she explained, if a little belatedly, to her father to survey the preparations.

'My father can afford it,' she confided matter-of-factly. 'And if he couldn't have, my elder brother would have stepped in and plugged the holes in the financial dike, as one might say——' with a smile ' — with sackfuls of francs — Swiss, of course. Er. . .' She hesitated, which was so uncharacteristic that Abigail stared at her. 'Abigail.'

'Yes?'

'I would very much like you to do me a favour.' With a disarming smile, 'Yes?'

'If I can.'

'You can. Your help is urgently needed in my work-room. I need you for a fitting.'

Puzzled, Abigail followed her down, and as her friend opened the door she halted, lips apart, eyes bright with astonishment and admiration. She found herself staring at the model gown that until now Martina had kept resolutely away from public view.

Arms flung wide, Martina announced, 'Here it is, the *pièce de résistance* of my clothes show. The climax, the star, peak of perfection that it is.'

'The bridal gown. Martina, it's fantastic.'

'It will certainly set the tongues wagging, Abby, which is my intention. I will make my mark on the fashion world with this, even if by that "world" I mean the country of my birth. The favour I would like you to do me, Abby, is to try it on for me. For last-minute touches, you know?'

'But——' Abigail looked around '—I thought you had two model girls to show the clothes.'

'I have. Andrea has arrived, but Henrietta is as unreliable as ever. She is late. Will you, *please*?'

'Can't Andrea try it on for you?'

'Her measurements are just a little larger than Henrietta's, whereas hers and yours are practically identical.'

'But, Martina, I——'

'OK, you will. Thanks a million. Now if you will go behind that curtain. . .'

'Martina,' Abigail exclaimed ten minutes later, 'it fits me like a glove. It's fantastic. I've never worn such a beautiful outfit in my life. The feel of the satin, the lace. . .' She ran out of words of praise.

Martina smiled, adjusting the long train, the pearl and diamond earrings which she assured Abigail were the real thing, likewise the pearl and diamond head-dress from which the veil frothed and cascaded. 'If you could see behind you—yes, turn and look over your shoulder in the mirror. There!'

Once again Abigail could not suppress a gasp. Embroidered from neckline to waist were scarlet

flowers with bright green stalks and leaves, finishing
with a giant scarlet satin bow.

'That should give the audience something to look at,'
was Martina's slightly cynical comment, 'and the con-
gregation, too, when the bride and groom are taking
their vows.'

She knelt to lift the drape of the hem, the folds of
the train, then rose, giving a short sigh of satisfaction.

'Thanks a lot, Abby. You would make a good
model,' she commented, head on one side. 'Maybe you
have missed your vocation.'

The warmth of the day lingered even as the sun
started its descent. The tallest mountain peaks, many
miles distant, towered above the closer ranges, gaining
an even greater majesty by their misty remoteness.

Soon the guests would be arriving and Abigail,
wearing the red dress that was Martina's gift to her,
walked to the terrace rail and dwelt on the blue of the
lake below, dotted with yachts, their white sails filling
in the gentle breeze.

She would never forget this place, she acknowledged,
nor the happiness, brief though it might have been, that
being here had given her. There was a dream-like
quality about her very pleasant existence here, but
dreams, she reminded herself, always came to an end.

She sought for the source of her curious premonition
of impending finality, but found no answer in the pearl-
blue sky, nor the white clouds that hung like chiffon
scarves around the nearer mountaintops.

'Beautiful, isn't it?' Raymond stood beside her. 'And
Abby, you're beautiful, too. I bet that's one of my
sister's creations.'

'It is. Raymond——' she covered her bare shoulder
with her hand '—does it reveal too much of me? I
mean, will people think I've gone too far? You see, I
don't know how your countrymen think on such
matters.'

'Don't you mean *countrywomen*? My *countrymen* will
think you're delectable, too attractive for their peace
of mind. Their ladies, well——' he smiled '—they'll

probably all be envious of. . .' His hands formed a shape. 'Get me?'

Abigail laughed. 'But I still feel a bit embarrassed.'

Liliane approached, casting a shy glance at Raymond. 'There is no need to worry, Abby. I agree with Raymond; you look very attractive.'

'We-ell, you too, Liliane.' Raymond leaned back against the rail, looking her over. 'Another Martina creation, I bet.'

Liliane nodded, glancing down at her dress. It was a very dark blue and crowded with sparkling blue sequins. Its shoulder-straps were wide, its shape clinging.

'Your sister believes in advertising her designs,' she commented with a smile, 'not just on dummy figures but——'

'On living, breathing ones,' he finished for her. 'I have to hand it to her, she knows how to market her goods. Not to mention promote her name and her business. What's your role this evening?' His interest in the slim young woman gladdened Abigail's heart. It was plain that *his* heart was not broken by Rolf's blunt statement regarding her own relationship with him, thus excluding his younger brother.

A little despondently, Abigail turned again to the view, without really seeing it this time. That 'relationship' was non-existent, wasn't it? As she had declared a few days ago, quite falsely, but out of revenge, it had indeed been a 'one-night stand'. There had been no love shown towards her on Rolf's part, but then he had warned her, hadn't he, right at the start?

'What is making you so unhappy?' Rolf, beside her from out of the blue, leant on the railed parapet. She was glad he couldn't monitor the sudden acceleration of her heartbeats. 'The present?' He gestured to the view. 'Or the future? Or——' with half-closed eyes he surveyed her face '——the past?'

How had he guessed? 'You must be a mind-reader,' she quipped, forcing humour into her tone. His appearance, so unexpected yet so welcome, had upset her equilibrium. His smile knocked her balance sideways, likewise her composure.

'So,' slowly his response came, 'what is so bad about the past that it brings such sadness to your face?'

Pressing her lips together, she shook her head. She would not, could not, tell him her thoughts.

He took her bare arm between his fingers—her skin came alive under the pressure of them—and turned her to face him.

'My lips are itching to make contact with all that my eyes can see of your semi-nudity.'

'It's. . .' She moistened her lips, whispering, 'It's only my shoulder and neck and. . .'

'And,' he took her up softly, 'almost. . .your breast. All of you—' he held her slightly away '—is asking to be revealed by a man's hand.' Fingers curled, he fastened on to the slanting neckline of the dress and made a downward movement. '*My* hand. If we were alone, *Liebling*—' his dark eyes flashed an unmistakably sensual glance '—I would not hesitate.'

Desire leapt within her; her flesh burned at the picture he was painting. She even felt a little breathless. Their eyes met and his smiled, although his mouth did not.

'Stop,' she whispered. 'Stop making verbal love to me.'

He laughed, head back. 'Later, yes?'

'No.'

His brows arched. 'No? We will see, will we not?'

'I'm not your woman.'

'Oh, but you are, Abby, you are.'

He walked away then, hands slid into the jacket pockets of his evening suit, a tall, distinguished figure that tore at her heart-strings, her love for him deepening by the minute. It was a love that had no prospect of being returned, and as she watched him go that feeling came to her again, even stronger this time, of the curtain falling on that episode in her life, like a stage play with an unhappy, bitter end.

CHAPTER ELEVEN

GUESTS had spilled over from the terrace to the sloping grounds that led down to the lake. More were arriving now, the level of chatter rising fast. Raymond, like his brother, had begun to mingle, their talk in the language of their countrymen.

'Hi.' A silky voice in a language Abigail understood only too well approached her. 'Feeling lonely? Rolf's sent me to stop you from feeling out in the cold.' Laura's sharp eyes went over her. 'In a dress like that, maybe you are. Sorry, that joke was in bad taste. That outfit makes you look as if you've got it all. How wrong outward appearances can be. Is it Martina's brainchild? I thought so. The bi— sorry, the naughty girl refuses to make me anything. Now why, I wonder?'

I could tell you, Abigail thought. I could be as bitchy back to you as you've just been to me.

'I wouldn't know,' she answered, nodding coolly and wandering into the crowd.

'Ah, Abigail.' With undisguised pleasure, she heard Anton Felder's greeting. 'It is going to be a good party, is it not? The musicians will arrive soon, did we tell you?'

'I was told there would be fireworks.'

Anton nodded. 'At the very end. And dancing here on the terrace. I did not realise ——' he glanced around ' —that the Felder family had so many friends and acquaintances. Some of them are my elder son's business contacts, and some are Raymond's friends, not to mention Martina's. Mine, of course, are in the older age-group, like me.' He smiled.

'You're not old, Herr Felder.'

He laughed, head back like his son. 'Do you know, there are times when I feel twenty years younger than I really am? People should know that; people should not

154

dismiss the older age-groups as if they had no brains, no experience of life, no *young* feelings. . .as if, in fact, they were *old*. But ——' his hand on her arm '—thank you for the compliment.'

His eyes strayed, resting with a frown on Laura, who had pushed through to stand beside Rolf. 'I wish,' Anton said, 'I wish my son had better judgement where the female of the species is concerned.' His head turned towards Abigail. 'I wish it were not Rolf and that lady, but Rolf and. . .' He sighed, omitting to finish the sentence.

Someone called to him and he looked around, clearly not wishing to leave Abigail alone. A shout brought his head round and he smiled at his daughter as she passed him, making her way towards Abigail.

Martina's eyes shone. 'Guess what? Otto, he's here. He kept his promise. And guess what, again? He might even play for us!' The piano had been moved on to the terrace. 'I told him to send in the bill for his fee, but that it might take us months to pay it, but he became quite indignant and said of course he would not charge. He would be playing for——' her voice dropped, her eyes outdid the sun's brightness '—a special friend.'

'Oh, Martina,' Abigail exclaimed, 'it must mean he's smitten with you.' She glanced over her friend's shoulder. 'I can see him from here. He's watching you. He's not talking to anyone else. Go, Martina, and put him out of his misery.'

'No.' Her friend drew herself up. 'I will play hard to get.' Then she collapsed into laughter. 'Abby, he's so handsome. And so famous, and so gifted. How can any woman ever keep up with him?' She did not pause for an answer. 'The dress show will take place towards the end of the evening, just before the fireworks. See you.'

Abigail began to mingle, wishing more than ever that she could speak the language of those around her. She caught Rolf's eye and her heart leapt, hoping he might break away from his group and join her. It was a vain hope, as she knew it must be, but she saw him call to his brother, gesturing towards her.

Raymond nodded and pushed his way through.

'Lost in a crowd,' he commented, 'is bad enough, but lost in that crowd where everyone is jabbering away in a language you can't comprehend. . .' He shook his head. 'You might just as well have landed on this planet from Mars. Yes?'

'Yes!' Abigail answered emphatically, smiling. 'But you didn't need to tear yourself away from Liliane.'

'That's OK. She had to go, anyway, to help with the model girl's make-up or whatever. Now come with me. I know where the best food is.'

The sun was beginning to sink behind the nearer mountains, but the air remained warm, the light staying bright, the terrace enhanced by the coloured lights strung around it.

Raymond led her to the long trestle-tables covered with spotlessly white cloths, the table-legs almost groaning under the weight of the delicious savouries on display. The sight of them, so varied and so mouthwatering to look at, made her realise how hungry she had become.

After they had consumed between them the contents of a plate piled high, Raymond made for another table, urging her to follow.

'Here, try this *fondue*,' he suggested, handing her a two-pronged fork, spearing a piece of cooked meat, and gesturing towards a *fondue* pot. 'Dip it in, then savour its taste.'

This Abigail did, making appreciative noises and turning her eyes up to the ceiling, at which Raymond laughed.

'Carry on spearing,' he urged, 'and dipping. The more you have, the more you'll want. Oh, I forgot to tell you. Be warned. Be very careful. Tradition has it that if you lose your dip in the *fondue* a forfeit has to be paid.'

Abigail made a face at that and vowed to keep a firm hold on her dips.

'There's *fondue Bourguignonne*,' Raymond explained, 'cheese *fondue*, which you've just had, and there's onion and herb sauce, and spicy tomato sauce. Not to mention all those out-of-the-world savouries over there. And desserts on that table. Plus wine; you must have some wine. Here. . .' He crossed to yet another table. 'You like chocolate? Then here's some chocolate *fondue.*' He took charge of her fork and speared a chunk of apple. 'Now dip.'

This she did, carefully lifting her dip from the chocolate *fondue*, but it fell back and she stared wide-eyed at Raymond.

'She's done it,' he shouted, thumping the air. 'She's lost her dip. Now for the forfeit.' He put aside her fork with his and seized her shoulders. 'A kiss as a forfeit, Abby. There's no getting out of it.'

A strong hand swung her out of Raymond's grasp and pulled her against a hard chest.

'I'll take the forfeit,' a male voice growled.

A mouth with which she had grown heart-breakingly familiar came down on hers with an impact that made her sway and catch at broad shoulders for support.

She was urged into a nearby corner and the kiss was intrusive and possessive, causing a weakness in her legs and a constriction in the region of her lungs. She found herself kissing back the interloper with a fervour that cut out all sense of her surroundings, not to mention whether or not the impropriety of her response might shock any other guest who might be looking, but of whose presence she was only dimly aware.

When Rolf finally let her go, there was a burst of applause from the guests around them, and a series of back-pats for Rolf from his male acquaintances that put the kiss firmly in its place — as a demonstration of his virility and his male dominance over the female of the species.

Nevertheless, Abigail's cheeks burned. She had kissed him back with such passion that it must have been obvious to all who watched how she felt about him. It seemed, however, that she had no need to be worried. Her surrender had been taken as yet another sign of Rolf's persuasiveness with the opposite sex, and was no doubt regarded by friends and relatives alike as a point in his favour.

'Now,' Rolf murmured, 'you can let Raymond kiss you if you like — then —' with a cynical curl to his lips '— make the comparison.'

So it had been sibling rivalry, too?

'No, thank you,' she began, then checked herself. She would play it his way! 'Yes, I will. Raymond. . .?'

Raymond needed no second invitation. The scowl on his face was transformed into pleasure as he gave her a forceful kiss that left her totally unmoved. She hid her lack of response behind a brilliant smile, which she raised in triumph to the face of the elder brother. The look in his eyes was so cold that she shivered inwardly.

Raymond's attention was distracted, and Abigail was left watching the striding, retreating figure of the man who had come to mean more to her than any other in the world.

Raymond stayed at her side for some time, acting as interpreter whenever a guest addressed her in German or Italian, or sometimes in French, a language she herself was able to understand much of.

The taped music which had been playing in the background for some time turned romantic and rhythmic, and people formed couples and began to circle the central space on the terrace, which had been left clear.

Abigail found herself dancing with Anton. 'You seem to be enjoying your stay here,' he commented, his eyes warmer, she reflected, than those of his elder son. Although, she recalled nostalgically, she had seen *those* eyes lit with warmth and compassion and. . .

'Thank you, Herr Felder, very much.'

'Good. I hear you play the piano.'

'Not all that well,' she admitted, laughing.

'But it must mean you like music. That is good, because we Swiss are very fond of it. Music festivals are part of our life. We have some musicians coming this evening. Soon they will perform for us. Ah, I have seen an acquaintance over there. Here, Rolf, will you take my place?' With a smile as he passed her hand over to his son's keeping. 'I am sure you need no persuading.'

Abigail pulled her hand away. 'There's no need for you to dance with me, Herr Felder.' She lifted a defiant face to his 'There must be many other women you would prefer to —'

'"Herr Felder" me again, *Miss Hailey*,' he grated, 'and I shall put you across my knee. No —' he added with lowered lids, 'better than that. I shall kiss you until you plead for mercy.'

'Herr Felder. . .' A young woman from the domestic staff waited as Rolf checked the swift passage of his mouth towards Abigail's. The newcomer, with an apologetic smile, spoke to Rolf in German and directed his attention across the room.

Laura was on the edge of the crowd, beckoning to him, her lips moving, no doubt conveying a message in his own language. The fact that he understood it even from that distance, and halted his steps, and Abigail's too, proved in her eyes how much more important Laura was in Rolf's scale of priorities, and how strong her influence was over his thoughts and activities.

'Please excuse me, Abigail,' he was saying. 'I have to go. I will see you later.'

'Why bother,' she called after him bitterly, 'when your lady friend is so willing and eager to satisfy your masculine appetite?' Her words were lost in the high noise level, as she had known they would be.

A fresh supply of food was trolleyed in, and Abigail took the opportunity to retreat to the rest-room. In her absence, the taped music had ceased and Otto Kaufmann had taken his place at the piano.

Silence descended on the enthralled audience as they listened to the golden notes that came from his fingers. He played short pieces, all of them classical, but every one of which was in tune with the happiness of the occasion.

Half hidden in a corner, Abigail spied Martina, standing, hands clasped, her eyes brightly adoring. The applause, Abigail was certain, could surely be heard by the occupants of the boats down there on the lake, so loud was it and so appreciative. Otto stood bowing, his laughing eyes swinging to Martina, who had emerged from her corner, hands raised in applause.

'Thank you,' she mouthed, and he bowed especially deeply in her direction. He slipped into the shadows, and the mood of the evening changed yet again.

A group of musicians were arranging themselves around the piano. They were resplendent in Swiss national costume, which consisted of black trousers and black short-sleeved jackets with bright buttons and red trim, while others had donned red waistcoats, all worn over white shirts.

One of the musicians held an accordion, another sat at the piano so recently vacated by Otto, while yet another held a double bass. A fourth member of the group coughed discreetly as if to test his throat.

The sounds that came from the musicians were melodious and cheerful and caused hands to clap and feet to tap. The singer began to yodel a song that echoed from the walls of the residence, over the sloping lawn and almost, it seemed, to the mountains beyond. The accordion's notes backing the song enhanced the amazing versatility of the singer's voice.

The pianist accompanied the other instruments, then branched out on his own for a while, playing piece after piece, light and happy, and with which, now and then, the yodeller and the other musicians joined in.

After that came the playing of cowbells and alp-horns, the sounds they produced, Abigail mused, almost causing the air to quiver and the ground to vibrate.

Abigail, standing alone as the performance pro-gressed, heard her name called and, turning, she saw Martina beckoning to her frantically. Making her way behind the spectators, Abigail found herself being tugged towards a side-entrance.

'Help, please, help,' Martina whispered hoarsely. 'The model girl who was to wear the star outfit of the evening has been involved in a car accident on the way here. Nothing serious, but she won't be able to come. Abigail——' her eyes pleaded '—I know it fits you. Will you. . .? Oh, say you will. . .'

'Not the wedding-dress?' Abigail exclaimed, wide-eyed. 'Martina, I wouldn't know how to——' her hands spread helplessly '—well, anything.'

'Who else can I ask?' Martina pleaded. 'You've already tried it on. Please, *please*. For me, Abby, for the sake of my business.'

'Oh, but——'

'I knew you would! Oh, *thank* you. But you have to come now. See, they are already erecting the catwalk and draping my fabrics over stands and fixing the floodlights. And, as you know, it takes a long time to get into that dress. The other models will be starting the show, taking it in turns to walk on, then walk off. While they are changing, I will address the audience about my fabrics and the services I provide.'

Twenty minutes later Liliane was adjusting the ivory satin folds cascading from Abigail's waist, flicking and smoothing and adjusting the bridal train. Then she helped Abigail with the make-up and pulled the veil into place. With a satisfied sigh, she inspected her handiwork.

Martina's voice drifted in from the terrace, and, ready at last, Abigail stood with her eyes closed, shaking inside, telling Liliane that she would hate to let Martina down, that she had never felt so nervous in her life, and, for heaven's sake, what should she do with her hands?

'Here,' Martina said, returning, her face flushed, 'this bouquet was specially delivered earlier for the wearer of the bridal gown to carry. Now. . .' She surveyed the finished product and silently clapped her hands. 'Just wonderful. All you have to do, Abby, is walk very slowly along the catwalk, pausing and now and then half turning—not a full turn, because the train would become messed up—for the audience to see every side of the dress, then advance to the end and stand there.'

'Martina——' Abigail began urgently, but her friend whispered,

'Don't worry, I'll be with you.' She seemed anxious and apprehensive and strangely on edge, all of which told Abigail how much her friend was staking her reputation as a designer on the presentation of the beautiful dress she was wearing. Determined to do her best for her friend, she allowed herself to be guided towards the curtain which hid the entrance to the catwalk, then Martina slowly pulled it aside.

'Now!' she whispered, and Abigail emerged into the darkened evening, the setting sun having splashed its afterglow across the pale blue sky.

There was a gasp of admiration, followed by a prolonged round of applause. Abigail steeled herself to do as her friend had instructed, half turning as gracefully as she could every few paces. There was another gasp as the onlookers caught sight of the bold splash of embroidery on the back of the bodice, followed by more applause.

Through the misty curtain of the veil, Abigail saw that Raymond was smiling, his hands raised in a show of encouragement and silent appreciation. Anton's face, too, was alight with admiration.

It was during one of the half-turns that Abigail saw Rolf. He stood, head high, eyes narrowed, hands in jacket pockets. He was not alone. Laura Marchant stood at his side, her eyes fixed on Martina's precious bridal gown. Was she coming to the decision that she would like the designer of the gown—her future sister-in-law—to make such a dress for her when Rolf had asked her to marry him?

Then Laura's eyes lifted in astonishment to stare at the girl who modelled it. Abigail noted, with a twist of her insides, that Laura's arm was pushed in a proprietorial way through Rolf's.

'*Meine Damen und Herren*. . .' Martina's raised voice caught the attention of the admiring audience. With the faintest sign of agitation, interwoven with an unusual display of apparent uncertainty, she then proceeded to address them in their own language, at which the eyes of everyone present swivelled to fix on Abigail's face.

For heaven's sake, Abigail thought, her steps faltering a little, what is Martina saying that's making them stare like that? Her eyes swung searchingly to Rolf's. She sought for the appreciation she had seen in Anton's smiles and in Raymond's pleased gestures, but this brother looked coldly angry, his lips thinning, his expression, revealed so clearly by the floodlights, becoming increasingly furious.

Pausing, as Martina had told her, at the end of the catwalk, Abigail felt the bouquet of fragrantly scented flowers start to tremble in her moist grasp. Rolf was looking at her as if he would like to jump up beside her and personally strangle her.

Why? she asked herself. For heaven's sake, *why*?

Applause, louder than ever, filled the air, dancing on the breeze, while the accordion player, seated in a corner, drowned the appreciative clapping with his rendering of 'Here Comes the Bride'.

Which, Abigail argued, growing a little tired now, was completely in tune with the occasion. Except that Rolf was moving, striding towards her, leaping on to the platform and taking her wrist in a painful grip.

Cheering joined the music and the applause, and it was under the cover of this that Rolf hissed through his teeth, 'Don't stand there as if you don't know what is happening. Martina is telling them that you are going to marry me. You and my sister, you were in league with each other. Don't deny it. It was your way of making sure that your place in the Felder family was so secure that you would be able to stay here forever.'

She could not believe her ears, and stared into his cold mask of a face, which not even the veil was able to soften. She struggled to detach herself from his hold around her waist.

'Rolf, I don't understand you. You're talking non-sense and so is Martina. I'm modelling this dress as a favour to her.'

'Oh, yes?' The disbelief in his voice made her heart

dive. 'You are no different from the rest of your kind. Out for wealth and position in life.'

He turned to the audience and swung her arm high. '*Meine Freunde, das ist meine zukünftige Frau.*' His raised voice rang with the passion demanded by such an occasion, as he repeated in English, 'May I present to you my future wife, Abigail Hailey.'

The cheering increased, the applause growing deafening. Below, Martina stood beside her brother, her smile wide, her eyes shining. Her hands were clasped above her head as if she had won a tremendous contest.

At that moment, all the sky in the vicinity burst into colour, and the entire audience turned to stare and smile. The air was filled with cracks and bangs and puffs of smoke as, overhead, patterns lit the heavens, shapes forming, flaring and dying, gold and silver and scarlet and purple. People gasped and shouted and clapped, faces lifted to the brilliant display.

These were the promised fireworks, except that now they were being used to celebrate the announcement to the world of the marriage of Rolf, the gifted, handsome and highly eligible elder son of Anton Felder, to an unknown — and moreover alien — lady, whose name was Abigail Hailey.

Oh, God, Abigail closed her eyes. No! As the lights flashed, the colours had mixed and merged, and the rockets had shot whistling into the now-dark sky, it had all become clear to her. The whole thing had been a trick on Martina's part, and Rolf clearly thought that she, Abigail, had been in league with her.

After all, hadn't she tried on the dress 'for a fitting', as Martina had pretended? And wasn't she now actually modelling it?

Then Martina's words the day they had inspected the house before moving in came back to her, ringing in her ears. . .'That woman,' Martina had said, 'that Laura. Somehow I'll get her out of Rolf's life. And I have thought of a way. Watch out, Laura Marchant. I am Martina Felder, well-known fabric designer and established leader of fashion in my own country. Miss

Marchant, who will never become *Frau* Rolf Felder,
here I come!'

'Please, Rolf,' she pleaded, 'you just have to believe
me. I knew nothing. . .'

Rolf, his face in shadow, was not listening. He put
aside the bouquet, lifted the veil, tossing it back, then
pulled her into his arms. He kissed her with such
apparent passion that she could do little but allow him
all the access he was demanding to her lips and her
mouth. Nor could she prevent herself, loving him as
she did, from clinging to those broad shoulders and
responding to that ardent, if slightly cruel, kiss.

At last his head lifted, his burningly angry eyes,
which only she could see, boring into hers. 'Are you
satisfied now?' he rasped. 'You are soon to be the wife
of a wealthy, well-regarded businessman. Have all your
ambitions now been fulfilled?'

The party was over; the guests had left. Abigail, seated
on a low stool in her room, looked at the hand that had
been shaken over and over again as she had stood at
Rolf's side, still wearing the bridal gown.

She could not put out of her mind the poisonous look
that Laura had directed at her as she had approached
them. Nor could she forget Laura's words to Rolf.

'How could you do this to me?' she had exclaimed,
her eyes having manufactured convincing tear-drops.
'You led me to believe it was I who. . .' A stifled sob,
then, 'If you think our business acquaintance is going
to continue after this, then you are going to be very,
very disappointed.' With another venomous glance at
Abigail, she had stalked away.

Trying to rid her memory of the incident, Abigail
shook her head. Then she touched the cheek that
Anton had kissed, heard again his words. . .'I am so
very glad that my son has come to his senses. I was
never so pleased in my life as when I heard Rolf
announcing his forthcoming marriage to you. Welcome,
my dear Abigail——' his arms had encompassed her, his
lips alighting on her cheek in an affectionate kiss '—to

the Felder family. It will be enriched by your presence
within it.'

She had tried to tell him that it wasn't true, that it
was a plot conjured up by his daughter as a way of
getting Laura out of Rolf's life, but Anton had turned
away, still smiling, deaf to everything but the happy
news that still filled his head.

Martina had not been in the changing-room when the
bridal dress had been removed. Liliane had helped her,
as delighted as everyone else had been at the news.
Everyone, that was, she reminded herself, except the
two people most concerned.

Although Rolf had remained at her side as the guests
had departed after the firework display, he had not
addressed another word to her. With a cool, 'Please
excuse me, I must get changed,' she had walked slowly,
head high, back to the house, Raymond darting to her
to lift the train.

'Would you like to bash my sister?' he had asked
with a small smile. 'Or do you wish me to do it? I hope
you will succeed in persuading my brother of your
innocence.' His eyes had held a certain bleakness that
touched Abigail's heart. 'No doubt,' he'd added as he
escorted her into the work-room, 'you know by now
how to twist him round your little finger. A man has his
vulnerable side, even my brother. You've probably
discovered the right way to stroke him to avoid getting
hurt by his hedgehog-like prickles.'

There was a peremptory rap on the door now and
Rolf entered, the fact he was there without invitation
not seeming to trouble him one bit.

'So you are to be my bride.' He shut the door with
his shoulder and strolled, hands in the pockets of the
jeans into which he had changed, across the room.
'Well, well.' He regarded her broodingly, his look a
cocktail mix of insolence and sensuality. 'It was such
news to me that I felt I had to come and inspect the
woman with whom I shall be expected to spend the rest
of my life.'

His steps slow, he circled round the stool, pausing at

last in front of her. 'It's a good thing, is it not, that my bride-to-be turns me on? That she triggers my basic male reflexes to such an extent that I feel the urge to take her here and now?'

Abigail, whose skin prickled at the coolly calculated words, shot to her feet. 'Oh, no, Rolf. No man is going to *make use* of me in that way.'

A step brought him closer. 'No? Just try to refuse me *my rights*.' He seized her wrist, but she jerked it free, at some cost to herself.

'You have no rights. I've told you that before.' Her voice had risen, which annoyed her, because it conveyed to him the fear that was growing inside about her ability to fight him off.

'Ah. . .' His eyelids drooped. 'But you have given me that right. This evening, remember? You, together with my sister, announced to the world that you are to be my bride, when all the time you knew, and she knew, that the so-called engagement was to be a private arrangement. You ——' he jerked her against him and the impact left her breathless '— broke the conditions of that "arrangement", so there is nothing now to stop me from breaking them, also. Which means that you will not fight me when I make love to you, because if you do I will not be able to control my very male instincts to subdue you in any way that brings about the result I require — your total submission to my desire, my needs, *to me*. Now. . .' His fingers caught at the sloping neckline of the dress and jerked it down, exposing one creamy breast. 'You will come to me, Abigail ——' his voice had softened, his eyes fixed on the swelling shape '— and I will make love to you.'

It was the narrow shoulder-strap now that had his attention, and it slid easily off her shoulder and he eyed the full shape of her, holding her wrists so that she could not use her hands to cover herself. Which meant that she could not hide from him her aroused state, since her breasts had hardened under his touch, his subtly seductive words.

She twisted her wrists and freed herself with tears in

her eyes, but she knew that she must summon all her forces of resistance to fight his onslaught on her emotions, to fight even her very love for him.

'You talk of "making love,"' she cried, pulling the dress into place again, 'when you don't have one atom of love within you, except love of yourself. No wonder the lady called Beatrice left you for another man. She must have stumbled across that truth about you, too. She must have discovered what a cold fish you are. Oh, you're an expert at seduction, of course you are, to get your own way, to get your way with a woman. But underneath that there's nothing there — no warmth, no feeling, and certainly *no love*.'

Her cheeks burning, she stood her ground, her brilliant gaze defying him. His face was a mask, the look he slanted down at her completely unreadable.

'Rolf,' she whispered hoarsely as he reached the door, 'ask Martina about this evening. I swear I knew nothing of what she intended to do.'

'Nothing? You had no inkling, not even the slightest suspicion of her intentions?'

Back came Martina's words: Somehow I'll get her out of Rolf's life. And I have thought of a way. . .

Not even then, nor even when she had been persuaded by Martina to try on the dress in advance of the show, had it occurred to her what Martina might have it in mind to do. How stupid she had been not to make connections. . .

He must have interpreted the flicker in her eyes, the flash of uncertainty, as advance knowledge on her part of Martina's plan. He swung round and left her standing, moist hands clasped, in the centre of the room.

CHAPTER TWELVE

'Is THERE still a vacancy for a waitress?' she asked the young woman in the office of the café, hoping that her English would be understood. It seemed that it was.

'I am sorry, the vacancy is filled.'

Despondently, Abigail turned away and took a seat at one of the empty tables outside, pretending to study the menu. She was not hungry, although it was early evening and she had not eaten all day.

That morning, as the sun was rising, and before anyone was about, she had left the house, carrying her cases, which she had filled with her belongings. She had left behind Martina's dresses, small gifts from Raymond, and, most of all, everything connected with the bank account which Rolf had opened in her name, including all the items she had bought with his money.

She had scribbled a note to Anton, apologising profusely for having had to go on her way, thus leaving him without an assistant.

Making her way in the town to Tourist Information, she had been told where she could catch the postbus. This she did, hearing the repeated warnings of its horn with a stirring of memories that were bittersweet.

A young girl approached now, pad in hand, waiting for her order. She must have taken the place of the young woman from Holland to whom Rolf had talked when they had come here together. It seemed years ago now.

Abigail ordered fruit juice. As the waitress turned to go, Abigail asked, 'Are there rooms to let here?'

'I will enquire for you.' A few minutes later the waitress returned with the juice. 'The manager says there are two. The smaller is cheaper.'

'Thanks.' Abigail smiled and paid.

She stirred the ice cubes with the straw, then drew on it, the taste of the pineapple pleasing to her parched tongue. Her eyes wandered, remembering the beauty of the hills, the sweep and dip of green fields, the trees straggling along the valleys and climbing to the summits, the mountains rising self-importantly behind them, remote and majestic.

'I would like to book myself into one of your rooms,' she told the manageress, 'for a few days.'

The woman looked at her a little doubtfully, then at her two suitcases. 'You have sufficient to pay for it?'

Oh, heavens, Abigail thought, do I look as down at heel as that? Then she realised that her request for work must have aroused the woman's suspicions. 'I have,' she assured the woman, picking up her cases and waiting to be shown to the room.

On the way they passed the piano which Abigail had noticed on her first visit to the place. She must have lagged behind a little, since the woman turned.

'You can play?' she asked. 'You wanted a job?' Abigail nodded, and the manageress told her, 'You could play the piano in the evenings for our customers. The pay would not be much, but it would cover your food and accommodation.'

Abigail expressed her pleasure, and that evening started work. She had been there for a week when a group of young soldiers came in. They grew merry and laughed a lot, going quiet when one of them drew the others' attention to her.

She wore a pale blue cotton top and matching trousers, and she had caught her hair into a ponytail, the style which she had found most comfortable for the job.

Their noise she had heard with relief. It was their collective silence that filled her with trepidation. The scraping of their seats, she reasoned, had to mean that they were leaving. It meant no such thing, she discovered.

They moved in a semicircle around her, and it was only with the strictest self-control that she prevented

her fingers from trembling and the notes she was
playing from grating on the ears.

'Hi,' one of them said, lifting her hair.

'What's your name?' said another, except that he
asked the question in German, although she managed
to translate.

'Got a boyfriend?' a third enquired, putting his hand
on her shoulder.

Her playing became faster, the tunes becoming jumbled. She hammered with her fists on the keys and
swung round, face flaming, eyes flashing.

'I am not what you think I am,' she exclaimed. 'Will
you please go?'

Taken aback by words they did not seem to understand, they were silenced for a moment, but one of
them laughed and took her hand, pulling her up.

'Will you leave me alone?' she cried, fearing all the
time that her resistance might make them even bolder.

A voice thundered from behind them, '*Sie haben
gehört was die Dame sagte! Lassen Sie sie in Ruhe! Sie
gehört mir. Verschwinden Sie!*'

Abigail swung round, unable to believe her eyes.

'Rolf!' she exclaimed hoarsely. 'What did you say to
them?'

'I told them,' he informed her coldly, 'that they had
heard what you'd said; that they were to leave you
alone. I told them, without politeness, to make themselves scarce. I also informed them that you belonged
to me.'

The young men, backing off, were eyeing the newcomer nervously as they resumed their seats.

'You're so wrong,' Abigail returned, her voice low
and intense. 'I belong to no one but myself.'

His arm moved dismissively. 'Will you please collect
your things?'

She stood stiffly, her body resisting with all its might
the pull of him. 'I *will not* take orders from you,' she
said. 'Surely my departure from the Felder residence
was enough to tell you that I wanted nothing more to
do with you?'

Even as she confronted him so boldly, she knew that if she were to give in to the tears that threatened and run into his arms, as she longed to do, then his power over her would be complete. And he would know it.

He seemed about to reply, noticed the intense interest of the soldiers looking on, and changed his mind. 'Look, get your things, will you? We cannot talk here.'

Abigail followed his eyes and silently agreed that, in that respect at least, he was right. But she wouldn't, *couldn't* for her own sake capitulate entirely.

'If I do, I reserve the right to come back. Or, more probably, go somewhere else.'

With which defiant statement, she did as he had commanded. Returning with her belongings, which she had pushed hastily into her cases, she found him in conversation with the manageress. The woman gave her a warm smile.

'If you had told me who you were,' she said, 'I would have accommodated you in the best room free of charge.'

Abigail glared at Rolf. So who am I? she asked him silently. He tossed a cool smile in her direction. So he had told the lady, too, that she, Abigail, belonged to him.

'My car is parked outside,' Rolf informed her, leading the way. He took her cases, placing them in the back, then, with a hand so firm that she could not disobey its command even if she had tried, gestured that she should get into the passenger seat.

Deftly he fastened her seatbelt and slammed the door in the locked position, striding round to slide behind the steering-wheel.

With consummate skill, he negotiated the many turns and twists in the road, once meeting the postbus on its way up, its musical horn giving warning of its approach.

'How did you know where to find me?' she asked tiredly.

'I did tell you recently that the Felder Hotel Group

was interested in the place. We bought it and we plan to extend it.'

Abigail admitted to herself that she had forgotten, and reproached herself for it.

'The manageress called the hotel. She had noticed the Hotel Panorama Grand labels on your luggage and thought she should check up on your credentials. Her message was placed on my desk and I didn't see it until my return from Zurich. I left early on the morning after the party.'

'So did I.'

He nodded. 'It was sheer chance that I missed your sudden exit. When I read the message this afternoon, it was like the final piece in a jigsaw puzzle falling into place. There were people looking for you at my request. I got there first.'

'You — you took your lady friend with you, of course,' she ventured.

'Lady friend? If you mean Laura Marchant, the answer's no. She has returned to base — to London — with no intention of returning here. Does that please you?'

'Why should it?' she asked rebelliously, feeling none the less a sense of relief at the news, although why, she could not understand. This man was no more for her than he appeared to be for Laura.

It seemed that the whole family, plus the staff, and Liliane, were on the doorstep to greet her. Bewildered, Abigail stared.

'Why?' she asked.

'Didn't you know,' Raymond answered, 'that the story's been headline news since you disappeared?'

'Business tycoon's bride-to-be vanishes,' Martina supplied, grinning broadly as if patting herself on the back for starting it all, and getting rid of Rolf's lady friend into the bargain.

'My dear, why?' came Anton's puzzled question. 'As Rolf's wife, you will have a golden future. Your every wish will be granted.'

'Yet you ran out on it,' Raymond remarked, his arm,

Abigail was pleased to note, around Liliane, who smiled brightly up at him. 'I wonder why,' he said with heavy sarcasm. 'Could it be that my wonderful *tycoon* of a brother has, for the first time in his successful business life, and through sheer sexist prejudice on his part, made a terrible misjudgement of, shall we say, someone's character?'

'Be quiet,' came sharply from that brother. 'Now if you will kindly scatter — please excuse me, Father — I will escort Abigail upstairs. She needs to unpack.'

'No, I don't,' came from her, then she cursed herself for the childish response. Following Rolf, who deposited her cases in her room, she found herself being forcibly ushered into his suite.

Catching sight of herself in the mirror, she saw how disshevelled she looked. Her restless nights showed in her face, her deep unhappiness more so. No wonder those young soldiers, she reflected, had had the wrong idea about her.

'We need to have a talk, you and I, hmm?' Rolf commented, looking her over, apparently unaffected by her untidy appearance.

'I can't think what about,' was her response, head in air.

'About personalities, yes? About, shall we say, characteristics? So,' he continued, after a pause, 'not only am I pigheaded, unfeeling and selfish — three of the *endearing* qualities which, according to my brother, you once attributed to me —— ' arms folded, he watched as she sank into a chair ' — I am also devoid of the ability to love? Except myself, of course.' He repeated her words with a twist of the lips.

She ran her fingertip along the arm of the wicker chair, her eyes following its progress.

'I take your silence as agreement,' he continued. 'In which case, I had better get out of your life, had I not?'

Her head tilted back and her shocked eyes met his. How could she tell him, That would be the end of my world?

Only by using attack as defence could she respond to

such a statement. 'What about your opinion of *me*? The other night, you insulted me with your innuendoes about my "ambitions" and had they been fulfilled, implying that I'd been after the "position and money" which you alleged—or so I was told—all women wanted.' Her eyes flashed. 'But what hurt more than anything was your belief that I had connived with Martina to pretend that I was your future wife. All right, so I had tried on the dress in advance—as a favour to her. To make sure it needed no alterations. It had to be right. It was the star of the whole fashion show.'

'And the girl who was to model it had been slightly injured in an accident.'

Abigail stared. 'So you know?'

'I know. Martina confessed the whole story to me. The girl was not injured. She was there, behind the scenes, in case you refused at the last minute to oblige. Martina's aim, as we all now know, was to get Laura Marchant out of my life. And you into it. In the former, she succeeded. In the latter. . .'

Abigail could only stare at him. He looked back at her, his expression unreadable. He moved to the door, opened it, and made a sweeping gesture. 'You want to walk out of my life? If that is your wish, please don't hesitate.'

She looked at the door, looked at him. If he felt anything for her at all, he wouldn't be giving her this option. He'd be pleading with her, wouldn't he, not to walk out on him?

If this was the parting of the ways, then she must accept it. With an immense effort, she stifled a sob, stood up, and made for the door. If only her legs didn't drag so. All she really wanted in the whole world was to throw herself at him and feel his arms close round her. . .close *lovingly* round her. At the door, she faltered, took a breath, and braced herself. Then she remembered the ring. Sliding it from her finger, she turned and held it out. He took it. So it really was the end. She must face the lonely future bravely.

A hand caught at her arm, swinging her round. 'Oh, no, you don't,' came harshly from his lips. 'Did you really think I'd let you go? I *want* you, you foolish girl, want you with all of my soul. Don't you understand?'

Something inside her made her struggle.

'Understand?' she cried. 'No, I don't. Wanting comes from a physical need.' He was holding her upper arms so tightly that she almost shrieked with the pain. '"Wanting" isn't enough. Never will be. And it's no use offering "love" because I wouldn't believe you. When you gave me this ring to wear, you made a condition: there would be no promise of love to go with it.'

'If I'd promised that love, at that time, would you have believed me? After all, we hardly knew each other.'

'But I. . .' She gazed up at him. Had he guessed?

'But you. . . Tell me.' He gave her a little shake. 'Tell me,' he ordered through gritted teeth.

'But I—I'd already fallen in love.'

'With my brother?' His eyes were dark.

'No, no! With you, with you. There, now you know it all. Does my confession please your ego? Will you now let me go? You won't want to have any more dealings with someone like me, who's *ambitious* and acquisitive and after wealth and posit——'

His mouth hit hers and she found herself gasping at the force of the impact. Hers was opening, allowing him access, her mind loving the way her body was responding to him as it always had done. She was no longer conscious of the pain of his grasp on her arms, which had somehow crept up to encircle his neck.

He was kissing her as though some barrier inside him had been breached, as though it was telling him he had waited long enough and his patience had run out.

'You will be my wife,' he dictated, speaking against her mouth as if his could not tolerate being parted from it. 'Tell me you will marry me.'

'Oh, but I. . .but I. . .'

'Need proof of my love? OK, Abby.' Huskily he held her away. 'I will prove how much I love you.'

'You love me?' she asked wonderingly.

'From the moment I set eyes on you when I lifted you from the road after my car had sent you flying. And afterwards, when you were recovering, I could not resist your bright, inquisitive eyes, or the music in your voice, not to mention the bonus of the rest of you.' His hands bumped over her shape, coming back to rest on her throat.

'Oh, Abby,' he said hoarsely, 'when I saw the bruises I had inflicted on you, I felt the pain of them as if they were mine.'

His palms slid down to her shoulders, his fingers making for the buttons on her blouse, unfastening them one by one. Then his invading hands found their way inside to caress and stroke first one breast, then the other.

She gasped as his lips took over from his hands, and her own hands, having pushed their way beneath his cotton shirt, came across his chest, her lips not far behind.

He drew in a breath, lifted her bodily, and carried her into the bedroom, peeling away the rest of her clothes, then divesting himself in a few fluid movements of his own.

'This is what *wanting* means,' he said thickly as their bodies came into searing contact with each other. 'This is the meaning of *needing*. . .and this,' he added as his mouth rediscovered the secret places of her body, and made her at last abandon all restraint, 'is the meaning of *love*.'

When, after a seemingly unending time of passionate movements interspersed with murmured endearments, he finally took her, she released a shuddering breath, then gasped for another. He was invading her body again at long last, a moment for which she'd been waiting for, craving for, for never-ending hours and days.

Her mouth rooted for his, bringing it back from pulsating places all over her. Her lips parted, inviting his total possession of her innermost self.

Her throbbing body had found the rhythm of the love he was giving her and taking from her, too, and the ecstasy went on and on until together they reached a shimmering, golden pinnacle, descending at last into a deep tranquillity and total harmony.

Rousing after a while, Rolf propped himself on his elbow, looking down at her. 'You take my breath away, my love.' His mouth muttered against hers, 'You're everything a man could ever want in a woman.'

Her arms lifted around his neck and she smiled up at him, eyes sparkling, face radiant. 'You're not so bad yourself,' she commented, laughing when his fist made softly glancing contact with her chin.

Some time later, having showered together, they sat, dressed again, arms entwined, on a two-seater sofa overlooking the view.

'There are things I have to do,' he murmured into her neck.

Her heart slipped a notch. 'You're going away again? To visit Laura, perhaps?' It hung with a surprising bitterness on the air around them.

Within the circle of his arms, he put a small distance between them. 'You are jealous? Of her? You cannot be, Abby!' His broad shoulders shrugged. 'OK, so she selected me as her quarry. That does not mean——'

'But when I first arrived here Raymond took me into your room and I saw a photograph of her there.'

'She gave it to me, complete with its frame. I put it there because I could not think of anywhere else to put it. Listen, my love. . .' He looked into her vibrant, upturned features. 'Never once did I give her any encouragement, nor did I ever respond to her undisguised, not to say somewhat embarrassing tactics to persuade me to take her up on what she was so clearly offering me. What she wanted in return was—dare I say it?'

'Money and position,' Abigail finished for him. They laughed together. She looked at him archly. 'At which point did you decide that I was not after those things?'

'Difficult to say. At first, much as I was attracted to

you, I wanted to believe that you were no different
from the rest of your sex. Then you began to get under
my skin.'

'Which was something you swore you'd never allow
a woman to do again. Or so Raymond told me.'

'He did? One day I'll *squash* him for telling tales. I
have to admit that your ability to get under my defences
annoyed me just a little.'

'Why did you offer me that watch?'

'Not——' his teeth nipped her chin and she yelped
'—to test you, as you so rudely alleged at the time.
Would you believe—as a gift? And, as I said at the
time, to prove that I was not, according to Raymond,
the selfish bastard you accused me of being.'

Her finger pressed against his lips. 'I did not use that
word.'

His shoulder lifted. 'OK, my insertion. Now——' he
lifted her aside '—there is something I must do.' He
went to a drawer and extracted a long, familiar-looking
box. 'Give me your wrist, *Liebling*.' He slipped the
watch into place, and she could not help but admire it.

'It's beautiful, Rolf. I can't thank you enough for
giving it to me. But you really——' His fingers on her
lips cut off her words.

'If you throw it back at me again——' he manufactured a look of menace '—I have ways of making you
accept it.' He lifted her hand again. 'The ring. You
threw that back at me, too.' He shook his head with
mock-irritation. 'Never before have I met a girl who
disdains to accept valuable items *because* they are
valuable. I will buy you a diamond or whatever other
precious stone you choose.'

'But Rolf, your mother's ring, I love it.'

He frowned. 'It is of little monetary value.'

'That doesn't matter. To me, its links with the past—
your past—are of far greater importance than how
much it might be worth.'

He looked a little dazed, found the ring, and slipped
it back into place. 'I have truly discovered a pearl
among women. Not a diamond,' he teased, 'because

that is far too expensive, but a beautiful, genuine pearl. Now come, my love.' His hand reached down for hers and he pulled her up. 'We must go down and announce our engagement—our true engagement—to my family.'

'Rolf. . .' Long-sufferingly he stopped to listen. 'If you—if you loved me——' the idea that he should was still so fantastic that it was almost unbelievable '—why were you so angry with me when Martina announced our "engagement"?'

'Can't you guess? It was because I thought you, together with Martina, had betrayed my trust. It was to be a private matter, remember, a family secret. Besides——' he placed a fleeting kiss on her lips '—I wanted to be the one who made our engagement public.'

'Having consulted me first, of course——' she smiled, head on one side '—about whether or not I wanted to become your wife.'

'Not necessarily,' he answered with a mocking smile. 'I wouldn't have accepted a refusal, anyway.'

She tiptoed up to whisper in his ear. 'Has anyone told you how arrogant you are?'

'Many times, my love, many times.'

At the top of the stairs he paused, turning her to him. 'First, let's get this clear. With all my heart, I promise to love you, Abigail Hailey, as deeply as I do now for the rest of my life.'

Her arms wrapped around him as she whispered, 'And I shall love you, Rolf Felder, forever and ever.'

As hand in hand they reached the hall, they found the family waiting.

Anton sought Abigail's hand, seeing the ring. 'The engagement—it's real?' he asked chokily.

'This time it's real, Father,' Rolf assured him. 'Martina. . .' His sister smiled in answer. 'That wedding-dress—we shall be needing it soon.'

Martina's hands clasped above her head in a victory salute.

Raymond stepped forward. 'If you will excuse me,

Rolf. . .' He kissed Abigail on both cheeks, then said, with a smile, 'Was that *brotherly* enough for you, Brother?'

Anton hugged Abigail. 'Thank God my son has come to his senses and it is you who are to be my future daughter-in-law.' He turned to his son, shaking his hand. 'I will tell you both a secret. We, Raymond and I, were in league with Martina on the night of the party.'

At which Martina's arms, which seemed to have lengthened surprisingly in the space of a few moments, encompassed them all.

LUCERNE — 'city of mountains and bridges'

Lucerne lies at the northernmost tip of Lake Lucerne, at the point where the river Reuss flows out of the lake, a lake which has been eulogised by poets and composers throughout the ages. With its well preserved mediaeval core and beautiful historic buildings, its elegance and its magnificent panoramic mountain views, the city justly deserves its reputation as one of Switzerland's jewels.

THE ROMANTIC PAST

The history of Switzerland can be traced right back to the Stone Age, but the first recorded inhabitants were tribes of people called the Helvitii in the north-west and the Rhaetians in the south-west.

Lucerne first appears in historical records as **Luciaria** in 840, a village named after the Benedictine monastery of St Leodegar. After the opening of the **St Gotthard pass** in around 1220, however, the monastery village began its growth into an important trading town, a stopping point for merchants, messengers and pilgrims on their north-south journeys. By 1450 the town already had more than four hundred inns and restaurants!

Switzerland can justly claim the parentage of modern tourism, for as far back as the eighteenth century artists, writers and wealthy people flocked from all over Europe and North America to view the incomparable landscapes and to experience the warmth of Swiss hospitality. Switzerland has a strong and thriving cultural tradition — the artists **Le Corbusier** and **Giacometti** were Swiss-born, and so was the writer **Jean-Jacques Rousseau**. Other Swiss writers include **Madame de Staël**, **Max Frisch**, and **Johanna Spyri**, best known for her children's story, *Heidi*; plus the famous psychologist **Carl Jung**. Switzerland was also an inspiration for artists from other countries; **Wagner** wrote parts of *The Mastersinger*, *Siegfried* and *The Twilight of the Gods* at a villa at Tribschen, just outside Lucerne.

Lucerne, or rather Altdorf, a village just outside it, is also the location for the most famous Swiss legend of all, the story of **William Tell**, the Swiss hero who is said to have been sentenced, for refusing to salute the Habsburg badge when they were in power during the late thirteenth and early fourteenth centuries, to shoot an apple off his son's head. Fortunately he accomplished this unlikely feat, and his son lived to tell the tale!

In spite of the Swiss people's modern way of life, many of the folk customs are living connections with the past. They range from centuries-old ceremonies commemorating national victories to popular pageants and processions relating to both the pagan and the religious calendar. On New Year's Eve figures dress up in fancy costumes and parade through the streets, symbolising the end of the Old Year and the time of darkness. In spring there is the old custom of **Eieraufleset** (picking up the eggs) in which the egg is a fertility symbol representing the victory of spring over winter. In autumn there are many vintage and grape festivals, especially in the wine-producing areas, and the custom of yodelling, which prevails in dairy-farming regions, appears to have originated in the evening prayers which have been sung since the Middle Ages by the shepherds.

Each area has its own local customs. Lucerne has its own **carnival**, towards the end of February. And on December 5th, the eve of St Nicholas' Day, the village of Küssnacht, on the shores of Lake Lucerne, glows in the light of some two hundred enormous transparent bishops' mitres cut out of cardboard and lit by a candle from within. This festival is called *Klausjagen* — 'the pursuit of St Nicholas'. If you are planning a visit to Switzerland, it's certainly worth checking the diary to see if you can catch one of these colourful customs or processions.

THE ROMANTIC PRESENT — pastimes for lovers. . .

To enter Lucerne is to approach the heart of historic Switzerland. The city offers pastimes for every taste: glimpses of past elegance combined with the buzz of modern living.

The city's unmistakable landmark is the Chapel Bridge (the **Kapellbrücke**) across the river Reuss. One of the best preserved wooden bridges in Switzerland, built in 1333, it has hanging from its roof rafters more than a hundred seventeenth-century paintings depicting scenes from the town's history. Beside it, an octagonal image of serene harmony and an imposing witness to the art of mediaeval architecture, is the thirteenth-century Water Tower (the **Wasserturm**), part of the original fortifications.

Take a relaxing stroll around the Old Town in order to capture the true enchantment of historic Lucerne. It's on the right bank of the Reuss and is a maze of charming, narrow traffic-free streets with old burghers' houses, and quiet little squares with fountains. In Kapellplatz is the oldest church in Lucerne, **St Peter's Chapel**, built in 1178.

From the Old Town it's only a short walk east to the northern shore of the lake, where you will find a series of broad tree-lined quays, the **Schweizerhofquai**, the **Nationalquai**, the **Carl-Spitteler-Quai** and the **Luzernerquai**, lined with shops, and hotels capitalising on the magnificent panoramic views of the Alps.

Go north from the Nationalquai and you will soon come to the **Lion Monument** (the Löwendenkmal), an imposing thirty-foot-high dying lion carved out of living rock, which commemorates the Swiss Guards who were killed at the Tuileries during the French Revolution. Mark Twain called the Lion Monument 'the saddest and most poignant piece of rock on earth'. Above the monument is the fascinating **Glacier Garden**, a remarkable relic of the Ice Age which brings ancient history to life.

If you feel the need to spend some time out of the city, an ideal excursion would be to one of the nearby **mountains**, where you can see some of the many varieties of Alpine flower. Take a cogwheel train up **Mount Rigi**, 'the singing mountain', or an aerial cable car up **Pilatus**, 'where you feel on top of the world', and experience the fresh, clean air and the absolutely stunning views. Or else try one of the many **lake cruises** available — you can even take a special Sunday morning 'boat breakfast' on the lake! There are so many experiences in and around Lucerne to make you forget your everyday cares — and concentrate on the person you came with!

You'll probably be feeling hungry by now, so it's just as well that the large variety of Swiss cuisine is both appetising and filling. The Swiss are great soup-eaters, and soups are often a complete meal in themselves, so that might be all you need for lunch. If you've more time, however, a romantic meal for two might consist of *Geschnitzeltes* — chopped or sliced veal cooked quickly in a butter sauce and finished with cream. This

could be served with *rösti*, a common Swiss way of
serving potatoes, shredded and fried in small cakes. The
potato, incidentally, is very popular in Switzerland — in
the German-speaking areas it's called the *Erdöpfel*, or
'earth-apple'.

Also popular, not surprisingly, are all types of fish,
particularly perch (*Egli*), pike (*Hecht*) and trout
(*Forelle*). And you're bound to come across some form
of *Bratwürst* or sausage — beef, veal or pork, fresh or
smoked, fried, boiled or grilled — so popular that it can
be bought by the metre!

Sauces form a major part of Swiss cuisine, and, taken
to extremes, what could be more romantic than sharing
a **fondue**, where diners dip chunks of bread, for
example, into a common pot of bubbling sauce; cheese-
flavoured is common, but there are many others, and
you might also come across **fondue Bourguignonne**,
where cubes of meat are skewered and cooked in hot
oil. There's a romantic tradition attached to fondue-
eating, too, so beware: if you drop your food into the
sauce you have to pay a forfeit — a bottle of wine for a
man — and a kiss for a woman!

A particular speciality in Lucerne is *Luzerner
Kügelipastete*, a puff pastry pie filled with diced veal
and pork, sausagemeat dumplings, raisins soaked in
Kirsch and mushrooms in gravy.

Finish off your meal — if you've still room! — with some
of the excellent pastries and confectionary available, or
with a Swiss **cheese** like the famous Emmentaler or
Gruyère or the less well known Sbrinz, the oldest and
hardest of Swiss cheeses, or Vacherin, or the soft green
Schabzieger, followed by Swiss brandy in hot sweet
coffee served in a glass and called *Kafi fertig* or
Kafi Buffet.

After lunch, if you're feeling cultural, there are many museums and galleries such as the **Folk Costume Museum** or the **Picasso Museum**; or, if it's the end of August, Lucerne plays host to an International Festival of Music. Autumn is also the season of markets; on a Saturday or a Tuesday, stroll through the open-air markets in the arcaded streets on either side of the river. For more serious shopping—perhaps for the watches Switzerland is famous for!—the main shopping street is the **Pilatusstrasse**. No one will be able to leave this city without a souvenir; the greatest keepsake of all, however, will be your memory of Lucerne and the longing to return.

DID YOU KNOW THAT. . .?

* Lake Lucerne is 24 miles long, and the bottom of the lake goes down almost as far as sea-level.

* Of Switzerland's 3,000 flowering **plants**, 160 are fully or partially protected by law. Fully protected plants must not be picked or uprooted.

* Switzerland's main **industries** include chemicals and pharmaceuticals, engineering, metalwork, leather, plastics and textiles, plus, of course, watches and foodstuffs.

* Lucerne, with 60,000 **inhabitants**, is the eighth largest city in Switzerland.

* The Swiss people's favourite card game is **Jass**, played with 36 cards in 4 colours.

* There are 4 officially recognised **languages**: German (spoken by 74% of the population), French (20%), Italian (4%) and Romansch (1%)—the remaining 1% is because of foreigners living there. Swiss French and Italian differ only slightly from standard French and

Italian, but spoken Swiss German, or *Schwytzerdütsch*, is quite distinctive.

* 'I love you' in German is *'Ich liebe dich'*. Or, alternatively, you could try saying *'Gib mir einen kuss'* — 'give me a kiss'!

POSTCARDS FROM EUROPE

HARLEQUIN PRESENTS®

Hi!

I know that the secrets to my past are here in France. But can I trust the mysterious Rohan Saint Yves to tell me the truth? And will that truth be painful?

Love, Sabine

Travel across Europe in 1994 with Harlequin Presents. Collect a new Postcards From Europe title each month!

Finish your yearlong journey with
TOWER OF SHADOWS
by Sara Craven
Harlequin Presents #1708

Available in December, wherever Harlequin Presents books are sold.

HPPFE12

Travel across Europe in 1994
with Harlequin Presents and...

As you travel across Europe in 1994, visiting your favorite countries with your favorite authors, don't forget to collect four proofs of purchase to redeem for an appealing photo album. This photo album can hold over fifty 4" × 6" pictures of your travels and will be a precious keepsake in the years to come!

One proof of purchase can be found in the back pages of each POSTCARDS FROM EUROPE title...one every month until December 1994.

To receive your gift, please fill out the information below and mail four (4) original proof-of-purchase coupons from any Harlequin Presents POSTCARDS FROM EUROPE title plus $3.00 for postage and handling (check or money order—do not send cash), payable to Harlequin Books, to: IN THE U.S.: P.O. Box 9048, Buffalo, NY, 14269-9048; IN CANADA: P.O. Box 623, Fort Erie, Ontario, L2A 5X3.

Requests must be received by January 31, 1995.
Please allow 4–6 weeks after receipt of order for delivery.

Name: _____
Address: _____
_____
City: _____
State/Province: _____
Zip/Postal Code: _____
Account No: _____
ONE PROOF OF PURCHASE

077 KBY

"HOORAY FOR HOLLYWOOD" SWEEPSTAKES

HERE'S HOW THE SWEEPSTAKES WORKS

OFFICIAL RULES — NO PURCHASE NECESSARY

To enter, complete an Official Entry Form or hand print on a 3" x 5" card the words "HOORAY FOR HOLLYWOOD", your name and address and mail your entry in the pre-addressed envelope (if provided) or to: "Hooray for Hollywood" Sweepstakes, P.O. Box 9076, Buffalo, NY 14269-9076 or "Hooray for Hollywood" Sweepstakes, P.O. Box 637, Fort Erie, Ontario L2A 5X3. Entries must be sent via First Class Mail and be received no later than 12/31/94. No liability is assumed for lost, late or misdirected mail.

Winners will be selected in random drawings to be conducted no later than January 31, 1995 from all eligible entries received.

Grand Prize: A 7-day/6-night trip for 2 to Los Angeles, CA including round trip air transportation from commercial airport nearest winner's residence, accommodations at the Regent Beverly Wilshire Hotel, free rental car, and $1,000 spending money. (Approximate prize value which will vary dependent upon winner's residence: $5,400.00 U.S.); 500 Second Prizes: A pair of "Hollywood Star" sunglasses (prize value: $9.95 U.S. each). Winner selection is under the supervision of D.L. Blair, Inc., an independent judging organization, whose decisions are final. Grand Prize travelers must sign and return a release of liability prior to traveling. Trip must be taken by 2/1/96 and is subject to airline schedules and accommodations availability.

Sweepstakes offer is open to residents of the U.S. (except Puerto Rico) and Canada who are 18 years of age or older, except employees and immediate family members of Harlequin Enterprises, Ltd., its affiliates, subsidiaries, and all agencies, entities or persons connected with the use, marketing or conduct of this sweepstakes. All federal, state, provincial, municipal and local laws apply. Offer void wherever prohibited by law. Taxes and/or duties are the sole responsibility of the winners. Any litigation within the province of Quebec respecting the conduct and awarding of prizes may be submitted to the Regie des loteries et courses du Quebec. All prizes will be awarded; winners will be notified by mail. No substitution of prizes are permitted. Odds of winning are dependent upon the number of eligible entries received.

Potential grand prize winner must sign and return an Affidavit of Eligibility within 30 days of notification. In the event of non-compliance within this time period, prize may be awarded to an alternate winner. Prize notification returned as undeliverable may result in the awarding of prize to an alternate winner. By acceptance of their prize, winners consent to use of their names, photographs, or likenesses for purpose of advertising, trade and promotion on behalf of Harlequin Enterprises, Ltd., without further compensation unless prohibited by law. A Canadian winner must correctly answer an arithmetical skill-testing question in order to be awarded the prize.

For a list of winners (available after 2/28/95), send a separate stamped, self-addressed envelope to: Hooray for Hollywood Sweepstakes 3252 Winners, P.O. Box 4200, Blair, NE 68009.

CBSRLS

OFFICIAL ENTRY COUPON

"Hooray for Hollywood"
SWEEPSTAKES!

Yes, I'd love to win the Grand Prize — a vacation in Hollywood —
or one of 500 pairs of "sunglasses of the stars"! Please enter me
in the sweepstakes!

This entry must be received by December 31, 1994.
Winners will be notified by January 31, 1995.

Name _____

Address _____ Apt. _____

City _____

State/Prov. _____ Zip/Postal Code _____

Daytime phone number _____
(area code)

Account # _____

Return entries with invoice in envelope provided. Each book
in this shipment has two entry coupons — and the more
coupons you enter, the better your chances of winning!

DIRCBS